KENNAQUHAIR

Ruth Hooker

illustrated by Al Michini

ABINGDON

Nashville

Kennaquhair

Copyright © 1976 by Abingdon
All Rights Reserved

Manufactured in the United States of America

Library of Congress Cataloging in Publication Data

Hooker, Ruth.
  Kennaquhair.
  SUMMARY: Having escaped robot-like from a holocaust six
children find their way to a livable valley where an old man
helps them become independent individuals, yet able to work
together.
  [1. Science fiction]   I. Michini, Albert. II. Title.
PZ7.H7654Ke   [Fic]   76-4799

ISBN 0-687-20794-0

for Bob, Todd, and Bradley,
Bob, Bill, and Geoffrey,
and Andrew

Chapter 1

They met along the road. The tall boy came from the west and the shorter boy came from the east.

They walked toward each other slowly. When they were close, they stopped and stared but said nothing. The tall boy looked back over his shoulder, back along the road he had just walked. Then he shrugged and shook his head.

The shorter boy did the same. He looked back over his shoulder, back along the road he had just walked. Then he too shrugged and shook his head.

They stood in the middle of the road, looking at each other. Their bodies were covered with shiny outer suits. Gloves covered their hands, and gas masks covered their faces. All they could tell was that the one from the west was taller, and the one from the east was shorter.

They continued to stand in the middle of the road for some time, not moving. The road itself was small, not one of the many-laned super highways. It had only two lanes, but the surface was hard, and there was a white line down the middle. From the north, another road of the same kind joined their road.

The boys turned and looked at the joining road. After several minutes of looking they started walking down the new road together. They walked slowly and mechanically. They did not look to the right or to the left. They did not know where they were going or why. All they knew was that they must keep moving.

After a long time they stopped again. They stopped because another road crossed the one they were on. There was a sign. The sign had the name of a town on it and a number, 2. The boys stared at the sign.

Beside the road where the boys stood, past the ditch, was a large tree. It was dead. The bark was gone, and the branches were broken. Beneath the tree something was moving.

It was a girl. She was dressed like the boys except that she carried a small satchel in her left hand.

She walked around and around the trunk of the dead tree. The third time around the tree, the girl looked up. Then she moved away from the tree, across the ditch, and onto the road.

Now there were three of them standing in a silent group.

They took the road to the left, heading west.

It was along this road that they found a fourth person. She was sitting beside the road on a rock clutching a rag doll sealed in a plastic bag. She was little, not quite school age but almost.

The tall boy, the short boy, and the girl stopped and stood in front of the little girl on the rock. She didn't look up. They moved on down the road. The little girl didn't come. They stopped and waited. Still she didn't come.

The tall boy walked back to the little girl, took her hand, helped her up, and led her to the others. After that he let go of her hand, and they all moved onward, the little girl too.

The four of them walked on and on along the road that led westward and upward. When they came to a gravel road with a stream beside it, they turned and walked along the gravel road.

It was here that they found another. He was lying in the ditch beside the road. They would have walked on, not seeing him, but he crawled out onto the road before they were past. They saw him and stopped. They all waited while the boy slowly got up. He was hurt. His arm was injured. It hung limply by his side.

They began walking again up the gravel road, heading north, higher and higher into the hills. The injured boy came too. Now there were five of them.

They walked on and on. Sometimes they rested, but mostly they kept moving, slowly and silently.

High up in the hills the road suddenly turned left and headed steeply downward. The tall boy, who was ahead of the others, stopped at the place where the road turned. The others joined him, and they stopped too.

The little girl sat down in the middle of the road. Then the boy with the injured arm sat down. Next the short boy and the girl with the satchel sat down.

Only the tall boy stood. He looked at those sitting in the road and shook his head. Then he looked at the road that led downward and shook his head again. Then he too sat down.

It was there that the sixth one, a girl, found them. She came from the west and found the five sitting in the road. She walked near them, and her eyes darted from one to the other.

The tall boy was the only one who looked at her.

In answer to the tall boy's look, the girl with the wild eyes pointed down the road she had just come. She shook her head. She waved her arms and shook her head several times. The boy nodded slowly, understanding.

Then the girl pointed in the direction the others had come. Now it was the tall boy's turn to shake his head. The girl looked around even more wildly. Her wild glances saw something, something the others had not seen. It was a path. It led north, away from the road that had nothing at either end of it.

She pointed and motioned for them to come. The tall boy rose first. He took the little girl's hand and pulled her to her feet. The girl with the satchel helped the injured boy. The shorter boy came too. They all followed the new girl with the wild eyes.

The trail led through silent woods. The trees were bare except for the pines whose brown needles had not yet fallen. There were no birds, no animals, just the six of them strung along the trail, moving through the dead forest.

They walked a long way along the rough path. As they walked along they looked only at the ground before their feet, except the new girl. She looked everywhere with her wild eyes.

So it was she who saw something that made her turn off the path toward a great wall of rock. The others followed.

When they reached the wall of rock, they found a split in it. The new girl went through the opening. The others stopped. Then they too entered the crack in the rock wall.

A narrow passage angled first one way and then another. At last it ended, and they stepped out onto a wide shelf or rock. They stood at the edge of the rock shelf and looked down.

Below them lay a valley. It was a small valley, entirely surrounded by steep hills. There was a long, low house in the valley and a barn and other small buildings. There were streams and a lake and meadows. It looked as though the sun were shining in the valley, but that was impossible. The sun never shone anymore. The sky was always dark with low gray clouds. But it looked like the sun was shining in the valley.

They looked at what lay below them. They didn't say anything. Instead, they silently started downward into the valley.

Chapter 2

The girl with the wild eyes led them down the steep hillside that had no paths. Around boulders, through stands of trees, and over streams she led them.

At last they reached the house in the valley. They stopped and stood still. The girl stepped up onto the wide, long porch that ran the length of the building. She walked across the porch and knocked on the heavy wooden door. No one answered.

The others sat down on the porch step and waited. The girl knocked again. Still, no one answered. She then joined the others, sat down next to them, and waited.

They sat in a row, waiting. They had stopped before along the roads they had traveled, but always before they had risen again to walk on. Now they had reached a destination and did not know what to do next. So they sat with their backs stiff and stared straight ahead, not taking in what they saw.

They did not see the barn nor the green grass nor the trees. Nor did they see the man and the dog come out of the woods at the far end of the valley.

The man was tall and he was old. He was hopping on one leg, helped by the stick he carried in each hand.

The dog stayed close to the man and ran around the man and sometimes stopped and looked up at the man and whined. Once the man stopped and stood on one foot, bent down, and patted the dog.

When the dog and the man reached one of the smaller buildings, the man stopped and leaned against the building to rest. From there he could see the house and the porch and the waiting children.

The dog bristled, but the man hushed him so he did not bark but only growled low in his throat. The man started hopping again. He approached the porch and stood before the six silent figures. The dog sat beside the man as he had been ordered, but he quivered and whined.

The man waited until the staring eyes focused upon him.

"You can take off your gas masks," he said gently.

Nobody answered. Nobody moved.

"It's all right. See, I don't have a gas mask. You don't need them."

Slowly all of them pulled off their masks except the little girl with the doll.

The man smiled at the little girl and held out his hand in a friendly way, but the little girl put her hands up to her gas mask and shook her head.

The man looked away from the little girl toward the others.

"Where did you come from?" he asked.

Nobody answered.

"You must be thirsty," he said as he unstrapped a water canteen from his belt and handed it to the first in line. "Here, take this. Drink only a little. Just a' small sip. Then pass it on."

He watched as they each took a sip and passed the canteen to the next one. The tall boy, who sat next to the little girl, reached out to take off her gas mask. She let him. Then, she too had a sip of water.

When they were finished, the man said, "You need sleep." With the help of his stick crutches, he stepped onto the porch and said, "Come."

At the door he stopped. "I think you should leave your outer clothing, your shoes, and your gas masks here on the porch." When they hesitated, he said once more, "I think you should." So they did. They took off their outer suits, their shoes, and their gas masks and piled them beside the door. Under their suits they all wore trousers and shirts.

The man led them into the house and up the stairs. They followed him slowly as he hopped from step to step, carrying his crutches in one hand, using the other hand to grasp the stair rail.

Upstairs, he led them down a long hall with many doors on either side. He showed each into a separate room off the long upstairs hall.

They lay down stiffly on their narrow beds with their eyes still open, not able to sleep at first.

When they did fall asleep, they slept for three days.

While they slept the man took care of them. He hobbled from bed to bed and fed them warm broth. When they cried and screamed in their sleep he comforted them. But they did not know because they slept deeply, the girl with the satchel holding her satchel and the little girl clutching her doll.

After the third day the man no longer came to their beds to feed them and comfort them. It was then that they awoke.

Chapter 3

When they woke up, the man heard them. The sound was slight, a soft whisper of bare feet on wood floors.

He wished he could get up and go to them. He had planned to be there when they woke. Instead he must lie in bed. His right foot, the foot that had been injured before the children came, was still angry and unhealed. And now his left ankle was swollen and purple because of a careless misstep that had caused it to turn.

He listened. Now there were more sounds, scurrying sounds.

The man cleared his throat and called in a voice as gentle as he could make it, "I'm here. At the end of the hall."

A hollow silence answered him. He called again in a more coaxing voice. This time there was a slight flutter of sound.

Soon they came in a group to the doorway of his bedroom.

"Good morning," he said and smiled. "Come in."

They entered and stood silently near the door, away from the big bed where the man lay.

He looked at them closely. Some of them put their hands to their faces feeling for their gas masks. They all looked bewildered.

The man asked them their names and where they came from. None of them answered, and they looked more bewildered than before.

The man sighed. Six frightened children and one old man who could not walk. How could they manage?

He sat up in bed. "My name is—," he stopped then started again. "You can call me Old Man," he said.

None of them spoke. The man smiled at them as he looked from face to face. He stopped smiling because he could no longer smile into such sad, serious faces. "That's all right. Someday you will speak, and someday you will smile." He closed his eyes.

A hollow, rusty-sounding voice said, "Olmun."

The man opened his eyes and smiled as he said,

"Olmun?" Again he said, "Olmun. That's good enough. That will be my name."

No one spoke. Olmun talked to them. He told them what they must do to feed themselves. He watched carefully to see if they understood what he said. Sometimes they nodded, and sometimes they did not. When they didn't Olmun repeated the same thing until they did nod.

When he decided they knew enough, he urged them to go and do what he had told them.

It took much urging before they would move toward the door. It took even more urging before they would leave the room.

As they hovered near the doorway Olmun said, "Go on. Go on." Then, to answer their looks of panic he said, "You will be all right. You have nothing to fear. Now is now, and now is all right, isn't it?" He paused and asked again, "Now is all right, isn't it?" Olmun nodded his head and slowly the others nodded too. He continued, "Good. All we will worry about is now. And now is the time to eat. Go on. Do as I told you." He made a gentle shooing motion.

Slowly, staying as near one another as they could, they went through the door and, staying close to the wall as they went, crept down the stairs.

Olmun listened to the soft noises of bare feet on the steps and clothing rubbing against the wall. He wondered what they would think of the big wood-paneled room downstairs, the low-beamed ceiling, the stone floor, the stone fireplace at one end, the woodburning stove at the other end, the long trestle table set with seven spoons and seven wooden bowls.

He heard the grate in the stove being shaken. He heard the scrape of a pan, the shutting of a cupboard door. Then he heard the hollow sound of spoons against wooden bowls. Olmun lay back on his pillow, closed his eyes, and prayed.

He prayed for the children and the valley and for the world, and then he prayed for himself.

He opened his eyes and listened again to the gentle noises drifting up from below. He heard the squeak of the pump handle and the splatter of water on the metal sink. There was a faint rustle of movement, but no voices. Then he heard them coming up the stairs. He sat up to be ready for them.

Olmun had asked for a bowl of broth, and they brought it. The one carrying the broth entered the room first and handed the bowl to Olmun. Then he stepped back to join the others before Olmun could say, "Thank you."

The man studied the group clustered at the door.

"Can you tell me your names?"

No one answered. "Can you tell me where you came from?" They still did not answer, and their eyes grew blank.

"That's all right," he soothed them. "You don't

have to tell me. I won't ask again." He smiled and nodded at each one in turn so they would know he meant to do as he said.

"What matters," Olmun went on, "is that you are here, and we are together. Now is now."

They watched Olmun in silence while he drank his broth, but he did not watch them. He was busy with his thoughts.

At last he said, "I will give you names. New names. Names you have never heard before. How is that?"

They nodded.

Chapter 4

Olmun glanced from one to the other. Then he looked at the short boy for a longer time. He was husky and sturdy. He stood calmly, both feet planted firmly on the floor. The short boy watched Olmun and waited.

With a quick nod as though he were agreeing with himself, Olmun said, "We shall call you Shabin. Yes. You will be Shabin. How do you like that name?"

The boy studied Olmun thoughtfully but said nothing.

"Can you say it?" Olmun asked.

In a hollow, cracked voice the boy repeated, "Shabin."

The girl with the wild eyes was the next to be named. She was slender and seldom still. Her fingers, her eyes, or her toes were usually making some slight motion.

Olmun watched her for a while and then said, "We shall call you Meeja."

The girl paused, then opened her mouth and said, "Meeja." She repeated, "Meeja, Meeja," and then nodded her head at Olmun. He smiled and nodded back.

The tall boy, who, in the beginning, had led the others, leaned his long, thin body against the wall and gazed at nothing. Olmun watched him. Finally the tall boy glanced at Olmun with unseeing eyes and then looked away.

Olmun said, "Your name will be Talig."

The boy didn't answer, only stirred and shifted his position against the wall.

"Your name," Olmun repeated, "is Talig."

The boy roused himself, looked straight at Olmun, and said slowly in a dull, faraway voice, "Talig."

Then Talig closed in upon himself once more.

Next, Olmun turned his attention to the girl with the satchel. She looked at him, then down at the satchel in her left hand. She lifted it and clutched it to her chest with both arms.

Olmun said, "I have chosen a name for you. It is Alew."

Alew did not repeat her name until Olmun asked her to do so. Then she said, "Alew," in a slow and wondering voice. Her attention was more on the satchel than on Olmun and what he was saying.

Then Olmun spoke to the boy with the injured arm.

"How is your arm?" he asked. The boy did not seem to understand. "It was your left arm," Olmun told him. "Try moving it."

The boy lifted his arm and moved it up and down, watching his arm as he raised it and lowered it. He seemed to be thinking about it, trying to remember.

Olmun nodded, "Good. Now, are you ready for your name?" The boy looked up, Olmun continued, "It will be Rydeck."

Olmun waited until the boy said the name himself, "Rydeck."

When Olmun turned to the little girl, she hid her face behind her doll.

"I have thought of a name for you," he said in a gentle voice. "It is Pummy."

"No," the little girl shook her head and mumbled into her doll. "No."

"Then what shall we call you?"

"Nobody," she mumbled. "Nobody."

Olmun held out his hand and whispered, "You

are somebody." But the little girl backed into a corner and sat down.

He shook his head sadly. "We must take special care of her," he told the others. "We will call her Pummy, and she will learn to answer to her name and know that she is somebody."

Olmun looked at them all. "So now we have names." They nodded.

The tall boy, limp and leaning against the wall, was Talig.

The short boy, who stood square and firm and fair, was Shabin.

Tall, quiet Alew clutched her satchel.

Meeja was the thin, flighty girl.

The boy whose arm had been injured had the name of Rydeck.

And Pummy. Pummy hid in the corner with her doll.

"Now," Olmun said, "it's time to get going."

Their eyes grew wary.

"I mean," he quickly explained, "get going to do things. Not go anywhere. We'll stay in the valley where it's safe until—well, don't worry, we're staying here."

As Olmun spoke he watched their eyes. It was like watching a mouse hole where a timid but curious mouse hid. If all were well, there would be a flicker of life. But at a sudden movement or sound of something unpleasant, back the mouse would slip, leaving a blank hole.

So Olmun watched their eyes. What he said next could coax them along or startle them into retreating even farther.

"I would like you to go down the stairs and out the big door to—," Olmun stopped. He started again. "The chickens need food and water," he said quietly. "Chickens are large birds that can barely fly. They live in a wire enclosure near the barn. Unless food is brought to them, and water, they will—uh—be very hungry and thirsty."

Gradually life flickered in the eyes of the listening children.

Cautiously Olmun continued. "First, you must put on your shoes. They are in the hall. I've cleaned them."

Their eyes showed neither fear nor understanding. Olmun instructed them once more. "Go into the hall, find your shoes, and put them on." He hesitated and added. "Bring Pummy's shoes, and, Talig, you can help Pummy put them on."

They left with less urging than before, but they still moved slowly and cautiously.

After they returned wearing their shoes and Talig had put Pummy's on her, Olmun began to tell them more about the chickens. "In the barn, the big building opposite the house, there is a sack of chicken feed. Walk across the yard, you will see it."

A long, low howl floated from the far end of the valley.

Startled, the children drew together, as close to one another as they could get. Fear and panic filled their eyes.

Chapter 5

Olmun laughed softly, but it did not calm the children. Soothingly he talked to them. "That was Howler, the dog. Remember him? His job is to watch the sheep. He's howling because something is wrong."

He told them about the sheep and the three little lambs, their woolly coats, the sounds they make, and their helplessness.

There was a scratching noise at the door downstairs. "That's Howler now," Olmun said. He searched their faces. "Could someone open the door for him?"

No one moved.

"Poor Howler," he said. "Poor lambs."

Meeja echoed his words, "Poor Howler. Poor lambs." She left the group and started for the door. They all listened to Meeja's cautious footsteps as she went down the stairs. Then they heard the heavy door open and scrambling paws on the stairs. Panting and wagging his tail, Howler came into the room

"Sit," Olmun ordered. The dog sat but whined and looked from Olmun to the door and back to Olmun.

"This is Howler," Olmun told them. To the dog he said, "This is Shabin, Alew, Rydeck, and Talig. Meeja you have already met, and Pummy is in the corner. They are going to help you. Now, lead them to the meadow and the sheep."

Howler looked at Olmun, thumped his tail on the floor, and whined softly.

"Go on," Olmun told him. But Howler did not move until Meeja said, "Come on." Then the procession started, Meeja and Howler leading.

Alew, who was puzzling over the satchel in her arms, took it to Olmun's bedside and handed it to him. "Thank you," he said. Alew said nothing, but she stopped looking puzzled as she joined the others.

Before Talig left the room Olmun said, "Talig, take Pummy with you." But when Talig tried to take Pummy's hand, she pulled away from him.

"Take hold of her wrist," Olmun instructed him.

To Pummy he said, "You must stand up and go with Talig."

Pummy stood up, and Talig headed toward the door, holding her by the wrist.

"Keep Pummy with you." Olmun told Talig. Talig nodded and left the room.

Olmun listened while they went down the stairs. They went faster than they had that morning, and the sound of Howler's paws was added to the sound of their shoes on the wooden steps. The thud of the door closing, followed by fainter footsteps crossing the porch, was the last Olmun could hear.

He sighed and reached for the satchel. Inside he found gauze for bandages, tablets for purifying water, a tube of medicine for cuts, bruises, and burns, a watertight container of matches, and wafers wrapped in plastic and untouched. Why hadn't Alew used any of them?

Olmun put some of the medicine on his sore and swollen ankle and wrapped a piece of the gauze around it. He examined the wound on his other foot.

Painfully he swung his legs over the side of the bed, but that was enough. He dared not try to stand. With his hands he lifted his legs back onto the bed and lay back on his pillow. Soon, overcome by feverish, pain-filled sleep, Olmun slept.

Chapter 6

After the door closed behind the children, they hesitated before leaving the protection of the house. But Howler led them onward.

They trudged along as they had on their way to the valley. But now, warm breezes swirled softly around them. The trees rustled. Howler went faster, so they went faster.

They came to a rail fence with a gate and a latch. Howler crawled under the fence so each of them crawled under the fence too. When they reached the brook, Howler splashed through the water. The children splashed through too, not noticing the stepping stones.

The meadow they entered dipped and swelled

gently with great, bare, smooth boulders scattered on the slopes.

It was to a group of these boulders that Howler led them. There, stuck in a crevice, a small lamb bleated high quick bleats. The mother stood nearby bawling. Howler began to circle the sheep and the six children anxiously.

Shabin and Rydeck stooped down and carefully picked up the frightened lamb, as Meeja reached out hesitantly to pat the shorn coat of the mother sheep.

Freed, the lamb quickly skittered away, joining the mother without a backward glance. Howler barked at their heels, guiding them down the grassy slope back to the other sheep.

The children watched for a while, and then they left to find their way back across the meadow to the house.

This time when they entered Olmun's bedroom, they stood a little closer to his bed and looked down upon the sleeping man. He woke, stared for a second, and then smiled.

"You are back," he said. "That's good. And now the chickens."

He gave careful, detailed instructions and gave each one a special task: the feed, the water, unlatching the wire door to the chicken yard, finding the egg basket, gathering eggs, and shutting the chicken yard door behind them. He carefully described how the chickens looked and how they would act.

Even though Olmun warned them, the children were not prepared for the scuttering, clucking, pecking chickens. Meeja was the bravest, which was good because her job was to scatter the feed, and the chickens clustered around her most of all.

The clucking, pecking chickens were too terrible for Pummy. She pulled away from Talig and went back into the house. There she crawled behind a chair next to the great stone fireplace and hid her face behind her doll.

When the others returned to Olmun, showing him the basket of eggs, he told them how to boil the eggs. They listened quietly and then went down the stairs.

The fire in the big iron stove was out. So they went up the stairs again and told Olmun that there was no fire.

Gesturing with his hands, he showed them how to shake the grate and remove the ashes, to find kindling in the woodbox and dry corncobs in the barn. He had to tell them about matches and how to strike them, about putting in kindling, about checking the damper and draft, and about lifting the lids on the stove top.

Returning to the kitchen to carry out Olmun's instructions, they stayed in a small group, going from one task to another like a school of fish. Out into the barn for corncobs they darted, then back to the stove. They remembered all they had been told and were able to build a good fire in the big stove.

After their meal was finished, they took two boiled eggs and two slices of bread to Olmun. He thanked each of them and called them by name: Shabin, Meeja, Alew, Rydeck, Talig, and, "Where is Pummy?" he asked.

They all looked startled. Talig answered, "Downstairs. The chickens." He tried to explain. "She went in the house."

"Yes," Olmun said, "chickens can be frightening."

They waited while Olmun thought. "I think," he said, "that we will not bring Pummy to us right now. But—." He looked at Talig. "Talig, you go to Pummy. Sit beside her for a while. Then, when she seems ready, bring her upstairs."

He spoke to all of them. "We must be kind to Pummy. And gentle. And keep her near us. Someone near her always."

"She can sleep with me," Alew said.

"Or me," said Meeja.

"That will be good," Olmun said. "Perhaps, for tonight, Pummy should sleep with Alew."

While they waited for Talig and Pummy, Olmun talked to them about the valley and the vegetable garden that needed weeding, about the cow and her calf. His careful, quiet voice did not frighten them.

Instead, it lulled them. They sat down, leaned against the wall, and almost went to sleep.

"Ah," Olmun said, "I forgot my own advice. Tomorrow will take care of itself. Now is now, and now you are tired."

He sent all but Alew off to bed. She and Olmun waited for Talig and Pummy. Alew cradled her head in her arms and slept while she waited.

Finally Talig came carrying Pummy and gently handed her over to Alew.

"You are very good with Pummy," Olmun told Talig.

Talig watched Alew guide the sleepy child from the room. At the door, he turned to Olmun and said, "I feel like Pummy—almost."

Chapter 7

The next morning when they went to Olmun's room, he told them how to make porridge for their breakfast. Downstairs they found the stove was cold because the fire had gone out in the night.

This time it was hard to start the fire. They made tiny flames with matches and kindling, but the fire would not start.

Rydeck went to the barn for corncobs. It wasn't until he was inside, gathering the dry cobs, that he realized he was alone. No one was with him. He looked around cautiously. The more he looked, the stranger the barn seemed to him, and the more alone he felt.

He left without looking back, holding his back stiff, as if something were going to happen behind him. Only when he entered the house did Rydeck relax. Even then he felt strange because of his all-alone trip. Although he said nothing, he thought about it often, and the more he thought about it, the less terrible it seemed.

The dry corncobs helped, and soon a good hot fire was warming the stove. The porridge was made and eaten. The chickens were fed. This time Talig and Pummy stayed outside the wire enclosure. Talig held Pummy's hand while she closed her eyes tightly and hid her face behind her doll.

After that they began learning about other things that needed doing. As before, they stood silently and listened to Olmun's instructions.

He told them about the cow and her calf. He explained how the calf had been weaned before, but, because they had not heard the cow mooing to be milked, it must have started drinking the cow's milk again. Now the cow must be led to the barn and put in a stall, but the calf should be left in the meadow. Olmun told them exactly how to do all that, how to be gentle with the animals, how to open gates and stall doors, where to find the rope halter and the hay and water to put in the stall.

Olmun looked worried. "The cow is gentle, but she is big. And the calf is frisky. We could wait until I can walk, but we do need milk now. Do you think you can do it?"

"Yes," they said.

Like computers being programmed, they had taken in every word. And, like machines or robots, they followed Olmun's step-by-step instructions without error. Working together, each did a special part until finished; they returned together to Olmun's room.

Now they learned about the vegetable garden. There was much to know about the small plants and how they differed from one another and the weeds.

Even though the vegetables were planted in rows with a stake at either end, they could not always tell vegetable plants from weeds. It was Rydeck who ran back to the house, alone, to ask Olmun whether the leaf he brought was a weed or a vegetable.

Sometimes, as they were weeding, they would hear the cow moo and the calf bawl. Meeja would go, alone, to comfort them.

So, as that second day wore on, the tight group that went everywhere and did everything together began to loosen.

In the evening Olmun carefully explained the milking procedure: finding and using the bucket and the stool, holding their hands to squeeze out the milk, and being careful of the cow's swishing tail.

Although Olmun worried, he need not have, for they came back from the barn with a bucket almost full of warm milk. It tasted good with their evening porridge.

The next morning Olmun asked, "Can each of you do a job alone?"

They hesitated. Slowly, first one and then another nodded.

"Good," Olmun said. "Many chores need doing. If each of you can do one by yourself, several chores can be done at the same time." He paused and added, "There are times, though, when everyone must work together. Right now the garden is overgrown with weeds and needs all of you."

Several were asked to do special tasks before going to the garden to pull weeds.

Alew was to make bread. She was to mix the yeast with warm milk and add that to the flour and salt. The bowl of dough was then to be left on the back of the stove to rise.

Talig was asked to tend the fire in the big stove. His job always would be to fix the fire so carefully that it would not go out.

Shabin was to fill the woodbox with stove-length pieces of wood. He would have to go to the woodshed, split and chop the big pieces that were drying there. Olmun showed the strokes Shabin should make with the ax and warned him about flying chips of wood.

Meeja, the best milker, was asked to take care of the cow and the chickens by herself.

Rydeck was to weed the garden by himself until the others could come to help.

Pummy was to stay with Alew wherever she went.

They left to go their separate ways, Shabin to the woodshed, Rydeck to the garden, Meeja to the barn, Alew, Talig, and Pummy to the kitchen.

After they had left, Olmun threw back the covers and swung his legs over the side of the bed. Slowly he raised himself from the bed and stood on his legs. For a minute he stood still, then took a cautious step. That was enough. "Not yet," he said to himself, "but I must keep trying."

Downstairs Alew mixed bread dough as Talig fixed the fire. When they finished, they went to the garden, taking Pummy with them.

Whenever Alew returned to the house to see if the dough had risen enough, she took Pummy. The rest of the time, while Alew and the others weeded, Pummy stood in the middle of the garden hanging her head and hugging her doll.

When the dough reached the rim of the bowl, Olmun told Alew how to knead the dough, divide it into loaves, and set them aside to rise again.

Talig fixed the fire so the oven would be hot when the loaves were ready. While the bread baked, Talig stayed in the house to watch the fire and Alew stayed to watch the bread. Pummy watched everything.

As they waited, Talig, following Olmun's instructions, churned butter. He turned the paddle of the butter churn and listened as it slapped the heavy cream. He listened for the swishing sound of the cream to change to a hollow gulping, for that meant the butter was forming. Just as he was ready to go ask Olmun what was wrong, he heard the sound he waited for.

Upstairs in his room, Olmun slept. He woke when the children came with their questions, and sometimes when he was alone. Those times he tested his legs and tried to walk with his crutches.

He wanted to leave his bed. He wanted to help the children. He wanted to see how the valley, the animals, and the garden were getting along.

That evening, when they brought him warm, sweet-smelling bread and fresh butter to eat, he told them that they had done very well.

"Even so," Olmun told himself, "tomorrow I must join in and help them."

Chapter 8

Olmun woke early, long before the children. Although he could hardly bear the pain when he stood on his feet, this was the day he had decided to get out of bed and go downstairs. He had decided, and he would do it.

Crawling on his hands and knees and dragging his crutchlike sticks with him, Olmun reached the head of the stairs. He sat down and slid from step to step until he reached the bottom. There he sat for a while and looked around. He was dismayed. The children had done everything he had told them to, but what he had not told them, they had not done. The table was covered with crumbs, egg shells, and the flour that Alew had used when kneading bread. The floor was streaked with mud from the garden.

Carefully, leaning heavily on his crutches, he shuffled across the room to the stove. It was warm; Talig had properly banked the fire for the night. And Shabin had filled the woodbox as he had been asked. But the butter had not been taken to the springhouse because Olmun had not told Talig to do so.

The children woke, and Olmun called to them that he was downstairs. They were startled when they saw him.. Olmun standing up was quite different from Olmun lying down. He was tall and he frowned. He sat down and stopped frowning, then he didn't look so different after all.

After they had eaten, Olmun explained about sweeping and cleaning. Talig did those things and took the butter to the springhouse. Meeja tended the chickens and cow, and the others went to the garden to weed.

When Talig left to help with the weeding, Olmun sat in the quiet house for a while, resting his feet on a nearby chair. Soon he lowered his feet, rose from his chair, and began shuffling across the room with the help of his crutches.

He stopped by the wall where the clock and calendar hung. Guessing at the right time, he set and wound the clock. At the calendar he hesitated. There was one page for each day. How many pages should he tear off?

Olmun looked out the window to see if the fruit

trees were in bloom. Noticing the beginning of blossoms, he tore off three pages from the calendar and paused before he tore off two more, then another. He studied the date for a moment then grasped his crutches and shuffled toward the cupboards at the other side of the room. Before he had gone many steps he had to stop and close his eyes because of the pain.

Just then Meeja came through the door carrying a basket of eggs. Olmun opened his eyes, looked at Meeja, and saw her feet. "Where are your shoes?" he demanded.

Meeja flinched. Without a word, she left, still carrying the basket of eggs.

"Meeja, Meeja," Olmun called after her, but she didn't turn back.

He stumbled to the table and sat down. Leaning his elbows on the table, he buried his head in his hands. That is how Rydeck found him when he came to ask about some leaves from the garden.

"Ah, Rydeck," Olmun said when he raised his head. "Go find Meeja. Tell her I'm sorry. I spoke crossly. Tell her to come back so I can explain."

When Rydeck came back he had only the egg basket, no Meeja. "She was running toward the meadow," he explained. Olmun nodded and sighed.

"Can you help me, Rydeck?" he asked. "Be my legs for a little while?" Rydeck nodded. "See that bin over there? Let me see how much sugar's in it."

Rydeck took the lid off the sugar bin and tipped it so Olmun could see from where he sat. Olmun frowned and said, "Now the flour." His frown deepened when he saw how little there was. "One more batch of bread," he murmured. "Then we'll have to grind some more. But the mill is too far for me and too hard—." He stopped and asked Rydeck to check other things, barley, oats, cornmeal, salt. As Rydeck opened each almost-empty container, Olmun's face grew more somber. The more Olmun frowned, the more frightened Rydeck became. Olmun didn't notice. He was too busy with his worries.

At last Olmun said, "That's enough," but then his gaze rested on the metal match holder mounted on the wall near the stove. "Is it empty?" he asked Rydeck. "Are there any matches left?"

Rydeck looked and said, "No. No matches."

"No matches? No matches at all?" Olmun lapsed into gloomy silence.

Rydeck, afraid to move, was still standing by the match holder when the door opened and the other children came in. Alew led the way, and in her hand she carried a branch of apple blossoms.

Olmun turned to greet them, but when he saw the flowers he said sternly, "Don't ever pick blossoms. Each of those blossoms would have been an apple. We need—." He stopped.

Alew looked surprised, then frightened. She stopped and came no farther. The others stood still behind her.

After a moment Olmun spoke. "There, there," he said. "The blossoms are picked. They are beautiful. Put them in a glass of water, Alew, and then we will have something to eat."

With slow, steady movements, Alew did as she was told. The liveliness with which they had entered the house had vanished. They were withdrawn and dazed, almost as they had been when they first came to the valley.

Meeja slipped into the house and joined the others as they silently fixed a meal of bread, butter, milk, and eggs. When it was ready they sat down, each in his place. They ate in silence, eyes cast down.

Olmun talked to them even though they did not seem to hear. "Meeja, I see you have your shoes on. Good. You must wear shoes, especially in the barnyard." Meeja didn't look up. Olmun went on in a softer voice, "I have been too worried," he explained. "I have forgotten my own advice. Now is now. Now we have milk and eggs and enough flour for one more batch of bread. There is the cellar—." He looked at the stiff children with their eyes cast down and said no more about the cellar.

"The matches are gone, except for the ones in Alew's satchel, which we must save. We must be sure the fire never goes out. And we can do that, can't we?"

Shabin looked up from his plate. He said nothing and his eyes were blank. He looked toward Olmun, then looked down at his plate.

Olmun went on, "Soon the garden will give us food. But there is a lot to do. Mulching. Cultivating. Fertilizing."

He picked up the leaves that Rydeck had brought from the garden. "These two," he said as he laid them to one side, "are weeds. Very pesky. Be sure to pull up all the roots." He held up the third leaf. "This is a bean leaf. Beans need poles to climb on. The poles—." Olmun shook his head.

"Now is now," Olmun muttered to himself. "I mustn't." He stood up. "Now I must rest. I'll go upstairs to my bedroom. Perhaps I came down too soon." He grasped his two crutches and made his way toward the stairs, Shabin following close behind. The others stayed where they were.

After Olmun sat down on the bottom step, he said, "Weed the garden this afternoon. The work will help you forget how sad I have made you."

Silently Shabin followed Olmun up the stairs and stood in the doorway until he was safely in bed. Olmun immediately fell into a deep sleep. He did not hear the children come up the stairs to go to bed. Nor did he know that they stoppped by the door of his room to look at him.

Olmun slept until some time in the middle of the night when he woke suddenly. It was strange. The room was lighter than usual, not completely dark as it had been other times when he woke during the night.

With the help of his crutches he went to the window and looked out. Then he looked up. He saw a cloudless sky crowded with stars.

Leaning on his crutches, Olmun hobbled into the hall and stopped by the first door. "Shabin," he called softly and knocked lightly. "Shabin, come." When Shabin opened the door, Olmun said, "Wake the others. Tell them to come. Downstairs."

Shabin did as Olmun asked. The six sleepy children, holding one another's hands, silently followed Olmun down the stairs. They waited while he leaned against the wall and raised the latch on the big front door. Across the porch and out into the yard they followed him. When he stopped, they stopped.

"Look," he said. "Look up. At the sky."

They looked as they had been told. Stars spread out and out and beyond and beyond in the deep depth of the cloudless sky.

They gasped.

Then they were silent, but it was different from the silence of the day. They continued to stare at the sky as Shabin began to sing. The music rose and fell, filling the listeners with exquisite pleasure and pain.

The song told of a starry night, a night divine.

When the last notes drifted away to join the stars, the children wept quietly. Pummy slipped her hand into Olmun's.

Shabin brought their blankets so they could sleep in the yard under the stars, comforted by their beauty.

Chapter 9

The next day the children woke with the sun in their faces. Olmun was nowhere around, but there were noises in the house. They gathered their blankets and went inside to find him busily searching through a cupboard.

"I forgot something," he said to them. "Something important." He limped to a big wooden chest near the fireplace, bent over, and pulled out a flute. It was only a toy flute, but it made music. He passed it around, and everyone took a turn blowing into it. They laughed at the squeaks each made.

"And something else." Olmun tossed a large, round ball into the air and caught it. "My grandchildren's," he explained.

"I forgot about games and songs. We need games

and songs." He was excited and happy; the children grew excited and happy too.

Olmun had to show them how to play. "When I throw the ball to you, Meeja, you catch it. That's right. Now throw it to someone else."

Olmun also taught them to play tag. But when Alew was being chased, she started to scream and scream. They stopped and comforted her and promised never to play chasing games again. Instead they played racing games, and that was better.

After that, life was different. There were still chores to do, but instead of carrying out their duties mechanically, they ran and skipped and called out to one another.

In the middle of the day, they enjoyed the good food that Talig, and sometimes Alew, fixed. They liked being together again after their long morning's work.

Afternoons they spent together. Sometimes they worked and sometimes they played, but whatever they did, they did together. They talked more and more. They told one another about things they'd seen and things they'd done. They asked questions. Sometimes they even worried a little. But Olmun would tell them, "There, there. We'll find a way. Remember, now is now."

When Olmun would ask Meeja, "Where are your

shoes?'' she wouldn't look startled. She'd laugh and go hunt for them. Sometimes everyone had to help her.

The day came when no one could find Meeja's shoes. They looked everywhere, even in the meadow where she sometimes went to visit Howler and the sheep.

"Meeja, what are we to do with you?" Olmun asked. "You know you can't go into the barnyard without shoes."

Meeja had to wear pine boards tied to her feet. To make them more comfortable, she spent hours testing and carving and shaping the wooden boards until they fitted the contours of her feet. She crossed a canvas strip over each instep and fastened them at the sides with nails. Now the clogs rocked along easily as she walked.

"They're better than real shoes," the others said with such longing that Meeja agreed to make them all wooden clogs.

As Alew watched the fruit trees lose their blossoms and slowly form minature, green fruit, she saw why blossoms should not be picked. Instead she found some wild flowers which she dug up and replanted on the slope behind the house where they could be seen from the window above the sink.

Olmun never again let his worries show even though he had many. Mostly he worried about food.

He told them about the cellar where other

provisions were stored: jars of fruit, dried beans and peas, potatoes and onions left from the last year's harvest.

One day he opened the trap door in the floor and showed them the steep stairs leading downward. The hole that lay below them was dark and scary.

"Talig, would you get a candle from the cabinet," Olmun asked, "and light it from the fire in the stove."

The flickering candle did little to light the mysterious depths. Olmun sat down at the head of the steep, narrow steps that were more like a ladder than a stairway. He attempted to slide down, then shook his head. "I'd better not. My legs are not steady enough."

He turned to the children who had backed away from the hole. "Could you go down the steps for me?" Olmun asked.

"I couldn't. I couldn't." Meeja sounded frantic. "I could never. Not ever." She backed farther away and then turned and ran out the door and stood in the yard.

"I'll go," Shabin said and Rydeck joined him.

When they came up from the cellar with two jars of peaches and some potatoes, they seemed glad to be back. But they told Meeja it hadn't been bad at all, only sacks and barrels and shelves, mostly empty.

Their next need was flour. They all went to the

mill. Olmun still could not walk very far so he rode one of the big plow horses with Pummy. The others took turns riding the second horse.

At the north end of the valley they crossed a flat wooden bridge then made their way along a rushing stream. The mill stood beside a pond that was fed by a steep waterfall.

Olmun showed them the gears and grinding stones inside the mill. He told them how to open the sluice to change the flow of water so it would turn the wheel which turned the gears that set the grinding stones moving.

Pummy watched with frightened eyes and covered her ears to shut out the noise.

After they filled a sack with the freshly ground wheat flour, they swam in the pond beside the mill. They stood under the waterfall and dove from a rock on the edge of the pond.

Before Olmun was able to walk about easily, he spent most of his time in the study. A door beneath the staircase led into this room. Shelves full of books lined the walls. Opposite the door was a window seat, and next to the door stood a desk and chair.

It was here, at the desk in the study, that they would find Olmun whenever they came to ask questions. He would stop reading or writing in the big book he called his account book and talk to them.

Sometimes he talked about the books. "There are all kinds of books here," he told them. "History, philosophy, science—." His words meant nothing to them. "Well," Olmun said, "they are here, and any time you want to read a book, you may."

One day Olmun gave Alew a book about herbs and wild flowers. "Now my wild flowers will have names," she said as she leafed through the book. "I'm going to go, right now, and look at my flowers and then look at the pictures in the book and find their names."

Talig, who stayed in the house more than the others, visited Olmun in his study most often. Sometimes Talig would take a book from a shelf, look at it, read a few words, and then put it back in its place. Gradually he read more and more until it became one of the things he liked to do most.

When Olmun was able to walk easily, he went from place to place and helped with the morning work. He showed Meeja how to crunch used eggshells and add them to the feed so the chickens would lay eggs with harder shells. "And," Olmun told Meeja, "remember to latch the door to the chicken yard." But Meeja didn't always remember. Then there was a scramble to shoo the chickens back into their yard.

In the garden Olmun helped put straw mulch under the tomato, pea, and bean plants. He showed Shabin, in particular, how to take care of the compost heap, and he showed them all how to thin the rows of plants.

Although Pummy seemed to know what was going on around her, she didn't talk. She helped; she watched; she listened; but she didn't talk.

One evening as they were all going up the stairs to their bedrooms for the night, Olmun stopped. "We forgot to put the beans to soak for tomorrow," he said.

They all trooped back down the stairs. Alew pumped water into a big kettle. Rydeck and Talig took a scoop and a candle and went down into the cellar for dried beans. Shabin and Olmun lifted the kettle onto the back of the stove where the beans would soak all night. Pummy watched all that was going on.

"There now," Olmun said, "we are ready for tomorrow."

Pummy looked at Olmun thoughtfully. Then she spoke. "Now is now," she said, "but we have to soak the beans for tomorrow."

Everyone laughed and Pummy squirmed. But their laughs were friendly, and Pummy soon lost her embarrassment.

On their way back upstairs they kept telling one another, "Pummy spoke." "Did you hear Pummy?" By the time they reached the top of the stairs, Pummy glowed with pleasure.

Chapter 10

One day after the morning work was done, Olmun gathered everyone around the trestle table. He had a large sheet of paper and a pencil in front of him.

"I'm going to tell you more about the valley," he said. He sounded serious, but he didn't frown. "What Pummy said is very true. 'Now is now, but we have to soak the beans for tomorrow.' What I mean is that getting ready for tomorrow is part of today's job. That is why we must take care of the garden. But we must take care of other things too." They gave no sign that they understood.

"Let me tell you about the valley." Olmun picked up the pencil and started to draw. "You know it is surrounded by hills and mountains," he said as he sketched tentlike peaks around the edge of the paper. "At the north end there are the waterfall, the pond, and the mill. From the pond the water runs down to the lake which is also fed by other streams. Here is the bridge we must cross and the road we must follow to reach the mill.

"Now, just before crossing the bridge there is another road that leads northward on this side of the stream. It curves away from the stream and winds back and forth until it reaches a pass that led out of the valley." Olmun paused. "It's now closed by a landslide. So, the only way out of the valley, that I know of, is closed."

Olmun paused again, and his voice was cautious as he asked, "How did you get into the valley?"

No one answered. They looked at him with blank expressions, the blankness of not remembering.

He tried again. "How long had you been sitting on the porch before I saw you?"

Once again they did not know the answer.

"Well, let me tell you more about the valley," Olmun said. "Years ago, when I was a young man hiking in these mountains, I found this valley. The buildings were here, but they were vacant. Whoever had built them must have left long before because there was no outside road leading to the pass.

"After that I could never find the valley again though I searched for it whenever I could. I began to think I had imagined it or that the valley was a dream. Then, seven years ago, after my wife died and my children had grown, I spent all my time searching, and I found it."

Once again Olmun picked up his pencil and started drawing. "Here is the house. This building I call the weaving house because it has a loom and spinning wheel. The woodshed is here and in the other end of it is a room with a fireplace. The barn is here, opposite the house. And this building," Olmun said as he drew a square beyond the garden, "must have been a smithy because of the forge and charcoal. There's a kiln too. Oh, I forgot the chicken yard, here by the barn."

Olmun looked up from the map. Everyone was watching closely. He went on, "I have spent most of the last seven years repairing the buildings, though they were in good shape because they were made of stone. I made the garden, planted the fruit trees and fields of oats, wheat, and corn." As he spoke, he drew in the location of each.

"I brought the horses and sheep," he said as he marked their positions, "and the chickens and cow."

"I got the mill to run. I sheared the sheep so there would be wool to weave and grew flax to be woven into linen, but I haven't done any weaving yet." He looked at them. "That is one of the things we must learn to do."

They all studied the map in silence.

"Ah," Olmun said, "I forgot something important. Important because it's dangerous. See the south end of the valley, the south end of the lake?" They nodded. "There is a sheer rock wall that closes the valley here. And the lake that looks so smooth gathers all its force and roars down under that wall and disappears." He paused and wrote Danger at the south end of the lake. "Stay away from it," he warned. "There's no need to go near anyway. I built a stone fence to keep the sheep away from the lake." He pointed to the place where the fence stood and marked it.

"What's on the other side of the lake?" Rydeck asked.

"It's barren and steep," Olmun explained. "But there is a path." He marked the map. "It climbs upward, along this cliff above the lake to a smaller lake. Just a pond really. But there's clay there. Someday we'll get some and see how our kiln works. I've never used it."

Olmun continued drawing. "The path then winds down to a little sand beach on the big lake where one gnarled old pine tree grows. The water is calm and safe there because it is protected from the main part of the lake by a wall of rock." He drew that too.

Olmun followed the path with his finger. "I wonder," he said, "I wonder if you could have, somehow, come—"

He got up and went over to the calendar. "Let's

see," he said more to himself than to the others. "I wonder when. I don't think so, but maybe."

They waited while Olmun studied the calendar and mumbled to himself. Then, noticing the day, he said, "Today is Sunday."

He went back to the table and sat down quietly. "I don't know your religions, but I know that in all religions there is prayer. Shall we close our eyes, bow our heads, and pray?"

They did as Olmun said, but before they were settled Meeja asked, "What do I do? How do I pray?"

Olmun tried to answer. "Be very quiet. Try not to think of anything. It will come to you."

Alew raised her head. "Sometimes when I'm in the woods hunting for wild flowers, I sit very still and see things I didn't know were there. When I'm quiet like that things come to me. Once a chipmunk almost sniffed me. And I see tiny things like spiders and small plants that I don't see when I'm just walking."

Olmun smiled. "That's what prayer is like. It is stopping instead of just walking. It is taking time to find out what there is that, otherwise, we would never know."

They all bowed their heads again.

Chapter 11

After the prayers were over, Olmun asked, "Would you like to see the other side of the valley now?"

They started out immediately. After they crossed the bridge, instead of turning left toward the mill, they turned right.

Here Olmun stopped and said, "As we walk along, if it seems familiar, if it seems as though you have been here before, please tell me."

No one understood so he explained a little more. "I thought perhaps you might have come into the valley this way, somehow. That is all."

They started walking again on the path that led upward and away from any growing things. It became narrow, steep, rocky. Then it leveled off as it skirted the steep cliff that dropped into the lake.

The view was thrilling and frightening. The whole

valley lay beneath them and the lake was at their feet. They felt they could fly out over the peaceful valley and touch the miniature buildings. But, oh, if they should fall from this height. They stayed close to the wall of the cliff and watched where they stepped.

Olmun asked, "Is this new to you?" They nodded.

Farther south the path began to climb again, winding through rock walls and ending at a small, placid pool. Tall, scraggly grasses grew around the edge of the water.

"Here is the clay," Olmun said as he stooped down and scooped up some of the slick, gummy stuff from beneath the shallow water. He dug deeper and brought up some clay that was more solid and handed it around for them to see.

They sat at the edge of the water, molding and shaping their bits of clay.

"This is like making bread," Alew said.

"But it doesn't smell as good," Talig reminded her.

Alew squished the clay and rolled it into a ball and then into a long, snakelike coil. "Are we going to take some clay back with us?" She asked. "Can I make things with it?"

"Yes," Olmun answered. "But first I want you to see the little sand beach. We'll get some clay on the way back."

He led them to the far end of the pond and down

a steep, twisting trail that doubled back and forth between high, solid walls until, abruptly, they stepped out onto a small, curved sand beach.

It was sheltered and quiet. The water lay calm and unrippled. The sand and tall cliffs around them were smooth. Only the single pine tree, standing gnarled and twisted, was rough.

Pummy asked, "Can we swim?"

"Yes," said Olmun, "but, see that wall of rock? Just opposite the beach?" They nodded. "Don't go beyond that. Behind that wall the water rushes down, with great force, and disappears beneath the cliff. I marked it on the map. Remember? It's very dangerous."

Swimming cautiously, they did not enjoy themselves as they did when they swam in the pond by the mill. One by one they left the water and played in the sand instead.

Rydeck made drip castles. That is what he called them. He showed the others how to dribble very wet sand from their hands onto the beach until it formed towers and turrets.

"Rydeck must have lived near a lake or an ocean," Olmun guessed.

Rydeck was silent, then said slowly, "Yes. I think I did."

After a while they headed home, stopping to gather some clay on the way.

Alew asked about making something with the

clay. "Maybe a bowl?" she asked. "How do you make a bowl?"

"I don't know," Olmun had to tell her. "But I have a book about pottery making."

By the time they reached the house, there was little daylight left. Olmun found a bucket for the clay. Then he noticed how dirty their hands and clothes were from carrying it.

"Hmmm," he said as he examined them. "Your clothes are wearing out. I hadn't noticed. Yes, you do need new clothes. Holes everywhere."

"Here's another hole," Pummy said proudly as she showed him a rip in her shirt.

The next day, after the middle-of-the-day meal, Olmun said, "Now we must see about new clothes for you."

He asked them to take the curtains down from three of the windows near the trestle table. They stood on a bench and helped one another slip the curtains from the rods as Olmun brought a box of needles, thread, and scissors to the table.

"I'm not much of a sewer," he said, "only patches and darns. The book I found about sewing seems too complicated, cutting out pieces in different shapes and sewing them together. Maybe someday. For now, we'll just do this."

Olmun took one of the curtain panels. It was sturdy material printed with small many-colored flowers. He doubled it from top to bottom. At the fold he cut an opening and explained, "We can sew up the sides, leaving enough room for armholes, use the tieback for a belt, and there it will be, a tunic."

Olmun slipped the unfinished curtain-tunic over Meeja's head and tied the tieback around her middle.

It looked nice and everyone said so. Meeja said she liked the way it felt.

Olmun cut neck openings in the other curtain panels. The taller children had shorter tunics and the shorter children had longer tunics. Pummy's would have been much too long if he hadn't cut off some of the material. The extra cloth was used for pockets.

They all sat around the trestle table while Olmun showed them how to thread needles, tie knots, and make stitches.

"There are enough curtains to make one more tunic for each of you."he explained. "After that, I don't know what we can use for material. Perhaps we should start weaving." He stopped to help Pummy untangle her thread. "Yes, I think we should start weaving very soon."

"I like sewing," Pummy said as she watched Olmun straighten out her crooked stitches.

Alew shook her head. "I don't think I like sewing."

But Talig said, "I do. I like making the stitches all the same size in a straight line, and I like seeing how far I have gone and how far I have left to go."

"I like tying knots," Rydeck said.

Shabin only grunted. He had to concentrate on holding the small, slippery needle in his blunt fingers.

"What I like is carving clogs," Meeja said. "It's faster. Or something. You can see better what you're doing."

"What I like most," Alew said, "is squishing things like clay. And shaping things. Can I make a bowl? Did you look in a book about making a bowl?"

"Well, no, Alew, I didn't," Olmun said. "First I had to see about clothes. That seemed more important for now."

"But bowls are important," Alew said.

"Yes, bowls are important," Olmun agreed. "We should learn how to make them. Perhaps tomorrow, Alew. But now we should finish these tunics."

Chapter 12

But they didn't finish their tunics even though they sewed most of the afternoon.

"I think we've sewn enough for one day," Olmun finally said.

So they put aside their sewing and went to the meadow to visit Howler and the sheep. They waded in the stream and ran on the slopes. Olmun took them to a far part of the meadow and showed them an outcropping of salt, a natural salt lick.

"It's important," he told them, "because sheep need salt. And so do we. It's here when we need it."

On the way home from the meadow they stopped in the pasture to see the horses. They came when Meeja whistled. Everyone patted the horses and fed them tufts of grass.

When Meeja led the cow to the barn for the evening milking, they all went along to watch. She let the others try, but none of them could do as well as Meeja, except perhaps Shabin.

The next morning, while Alew mixed a batch of bread, Olmun found the book about pottery making for her. Then Alew and Olmun took the book and the bucket of clay to the smithy.

"Bowls are important, aren't they?" she asked Olmun.

"Yes, they are important," he answered. "Bowls and crocks break, and I'm sure that someday we'll be very glad that you learned how to make more."

At the smithy, Olmun put a large board on a bench where Alew could work with the clay. They examined the clay and consulted the book. Together they read the instructions step by step.

"This will take a long time," Olmun said.

Alew didn't mind, but she did worry about the bread that she had left to rise.

"I'll ask Talig to finish the bread," Olmun said. "I should go now anyway to see about weaving." But on the way to the house he met Shabin carrying an armload of wood "This is the last of the wood, except for some poles and logs on the drying racks in the woodshed," Shabin said.

"Don't use those," Olmun told him. "I'm saving them. We'll have to chop down a tree for more firewood. There are trees in the woods that I've girdled so they'd be dead when they were needed."

At the house, Shabin filled the woodbox in the kitchen, and Olmun asked Talig to finish the bread for Alew. Then they got axes from the woodshed and went into the woods.

As they took turns chopping around the base of the tree they selected, Olmun explained how and where to chop so the tree would fall in the direction they wanted.

Leaving Shabin to chop off the limbs and smaller branches, Olmun finally went to the weaving house.

At the middle-of-the-day meal, there was a lot to talk about. Afterwards, no one wanted to settle down to sewing tunics. They wanted to see all the different things that had been started that morning.

First they went to the woods to see the tree that Shabin and Olmun had chopped down. Impressed with the great fallen tree, they climbed on it and walked along the trunk. They helped carry the many branches Shabin had chopped off to the woodshed, and from there they went to the smithy to see Alew's bowl. They all admired the bowl, and Alew was pleased.

"It's not as big as the bowl we use for bread," she apologized. "And it's not all done. But in two days it can be fired. Then, after that, it'll be done."

"I'll help you when that time comes," Olmun said. "We can give it a salt glaze. It should be very nice."

Next they went to the weaving house. Olmun showed them a book about weaving wool into cloth. They looked at the many instructions and sketches and decided it was a long, complicated procedure to make wool into cloth.

"We can do it," Olmun said. "Step by step, one step at a time."

Since the wool had been washed before it was stored, it was ready to be carded and spun. Olmun showed them how to handle the cards and the spinning wheel.

"As soon as we have made enough yarn," he said, "the loom can be strung, and then we can start weaving."

They spent the rest of the afternoon working with the wool. When they noticed the shadows lengthening and evening approaching, they were surprised and sorry that the day was coming to an end, especially Rydeck.

"Tomorrow may I help some more?" he asked. "May I help string the loom?"

Because they had stayed so long at the weaving house, there wasn't enough light left to sew on their tunics. But Talig said, "That's all right. I'll do the sewing tomorrow. I can sew while things cook. I can finish them all. I like to sew."

Except for Pummy, they now began to spend their days a little differently than they had before. Pummy, however, still went from place to place while she watched or helped wherever she went.

Shabin spent most of his time in the woods, chopping and carrying branches to the woodshed. Meeja took complete care of the animals and the barn and, when free, she carved clogs for everyone.

Rydeck helped Olmun in the weaving house. Talig spent almost all his time in the house, while Alew spent less time there and more time in the garden.

The blossoms on the peas and beans and squash were as beautiful to Alew as her wild flowers. When the blossoms withered or fell, she marveled at the tiny, tiny vegetables they left behind and watched excitedly as they grew larger, little by little. Sometimes Alew went to look at her bowl drying in the smithy. When the time came, Olmun built a charcoal fire in the kiln and helped Alew put her bowl inside. Then she had to wait once more.

The lettuce, chard, onions, and beet greens were ready for her to pick and take to the house for Talig to wash and prepare for their meals. Talig was always there. He sewed on the tunics when he wasn't busy sweeping, tending the fire, or cooking. Sometimes he read while he stirred soup or churned butter. And sometimes he sat on the porch step in silence with his hands empty. It looked as though he were doing nothing, but he was doing something.

One day he told the others about a poem he had made up, and he recited it for them.

73

"There is a valley
Where many streams flow
And many things grow
And people are friends."

Everyone liked Talig's poem. Shabin made a tune for the words, and it became the song they most often sang.

Chapter 13

As the days went by, their work progressed. Talig finished the tunics, and Meeja finished the clogs.

Olmun and Rydeck learned to weave. When Rydeck was able to work the loom by himself, Olmun turned his attention to the flax that was stored in the loft of the weaving house. "We can make strong, fine linen thread from these fibers," he said. "And the seeds of these plants can be pressed to make linseed oil. We can make soap from that."

"Do we need soap?" Meeja asked.

"Not yet. But we will," Olmun told her. "We should start now to experiment so we'll be ready."

"Soap? Soap?" Alew said. "I know something." From the pocket of her tunic she took the book about wild flowers and started leafing through it. "Here it is. A plant that can be used for soap. Bouncing Bet. I'll look for it."

"How can you wash dishes with a plant?" Talig wondered.

"I don't know," she answered. "We'll experiment."

Everyone went to see Alew take her bowl out of the kiln, but when the door was opened, they found the bowl broken, lying on the rack in two pieces. "I did want it done," she said. "I did want it finished. I wanted to see it and use it and have it."

"There, there," Olmun said. "You can make another bowl. There's more clay."

"Yes, only—," Alew began, but Talig interrupted. "Why did it break?" he asked. "Just sitting in the kiln, how could it break?"

"Maybe there was an air bubble," Olmun answered.

"Maybe I didn't squish the clay enough." Alew said. "That's what I'll do next time. Maybe I hurried too much. I'm going to make another bowl and, this time, be more careful."

But she couldn't begin another bowl right away. There were too many vegetables to be picked and other things to do.

When Shabin finished chopping the limbs from the tree trunk, everyone went to haul it to the woodshed. Meeja brought the horses, and Olmun brought the harnesses and chain. Shabin, because it was his tree, and Meeja, because she loved the horses, helped the most. She called the horses Girl and Boy, as Olmun did. But then she asked, "Don't they have names?"

"I know their names," Pummy said.

"You do?" Olmun questioned.

"Yes, their names are Girl and Boy."

"That's what I've been calling them," Olmun said, "but they do have other names." He paused. "My grandchildren gave them names." He paused again, "Their names are George and Jane."

"I've heard these names before," Talig said. "They're people names."

"Yes, they are," Olmun said. "I didn't tell you before because—well, I didn't want to say a name that might make you sad. That's why I gave you names you never heard before. Would you rather have regular names?"

Shabin was the first to answer. "No," he said, "I like the name Shabin." The others also liked the names Olmun had given them.

Meeja guided the horses as they pulled their heavy load to the woodshed. Everyone else followed behind and called the horses George and Jane.

The next time they went to the mill they hitched George and Jane to the flat hay wagon, and Olmun let each one have a turn holding the reins.

"Today," he said when they reached the mill, "we'll grind some corn too and have pancakes for supper."

"And swim," shouted Pummy who was learning how.

"Yes, and swim," Olmun told her.

On the way home they stopped at the strawberry patch. But there were no ripe berries. A few were slightly pink, but that was all.

"In a few days," Olmun promised, "we'll have a strawberry feast."

"I remember strawberries," Shabin said as he examined a pink berry he found under a leaf. Then he added, "I think."

"I don't remember," Talig said, "but I like the word *strawberries*." He made up a sort of poem, right then:

"Strawberries, strawberries, strawberries,
Strawberries, strawberries, strawberries,
And pancakes to eat."

"Strawberries?" Rydeck said. "They're berries, aren't they? Can't we use berries to dye yarn?"

"Yes, they're berries," Olmun replied. "And berries are used for dying wool, but I don't believe strawberries can be used. Pokeberries and blackberries, I remember reading about. They make red."

"Red?" Meeja said. "I love red. I remember I used to have a red—." She stopped talking and looked puzzled. Then she added, "Well, I remember, sort of."

"Yes," Talig said, "I think I remember things.

Little bits. Little pieces. And then I think maybe I don't remember after all.''

More and more they began to recall bits and pieces of things. But not everything. They didn't remember how they had come into the valley— until one day.

Shabin had gone to the barnyard to fill a wheelbarrow with manure for the garden and the compost heap. When he went into the barn for a pitchfork, he noticed something he had not seen before. In the out-of-the-way corner where implements and harnesses were kept was a round metal barrel. He took off the lid and inside found a jumble of thin, shiny plastic suits and gas masks.

He put the lid back and went on about his work, slowly and thoughtfully. He said nothing to anyone.

At the middle-of-the-day meal, although Shabin stared steadily at his plate, he ate without knowing what he ate, until at last he looked up from his plate and said, "I know how we came into the valley."

They all stopped eating. "Do you?" Olmun asked cautiously.

"Yes," Shabin replied. "We came through a narrow place in the mountain."

"A narrow place in the mountain?" Olmun repeated.

Shabin nodded.

Olmun paused a long time then he asked, in a soft voice, barely above a whisper, "Where?"

"I think," Shabin said, trying to remember, "it was high up."

"We saw the house down below," Alew said.

"And the lake," Meeja remembered.

"Did we?" Rydeck asked. Shabin, Meeja, Talig, and Alew all said, "Yes."

Olmun got the map from the study and spread it out on the table for them to see. He asked Meeja, "Was the lake nearest?"

Meeja frowned and said, "No," but she didn't sound sure.

"The house was nearest," Alew said with certainity.

"So it was on the west side that you came in," Olmun said. He studied the map some more. "If it were here," he said, pointing to the northern end of the west side, "the woods would have blocked the view of the house. Did you see anything else?"

"The meadow and the sheep," Shabin said.

"That helps," Olmun told him. "That lake is long, but if we line up the sheep with the house and the lake perhaps we can find it."

But Alew said, "No, we saw the horses."

Olmun studied the map some more. "Did you come down through woods?" he asked.

They only remembered being on the ledge and then sitting on the porch step.

Olmun asked nothing more about the way they had entered the valley, but when they were ready to leave the table he said, "I think the berries are ready to be picked today. Can you go alone to the strawberry patch?"

They said that they could, so they gathered their baskets, and started across the yard.

"Wait," Olmun called to them. "Come back for a minute. I want to show you something." He was busy unwinding rope from a cleat on one of the porch posts when they reached him. He pointed upward, to the porch roof. "See that bell?"

They saw a large iron bell mounted between two wooden struts.

"I think it was once used as a dinner bell. I never used it because it makes too loud a noise for our quiet valley."

Olmun pulled the rope and a loud clang rang out. Pummy covered her ears.

"It is loud, isn't it?" Olmun said. They all nodded in agreement. "I think you should know about the bell in case there's an emergency. But ring it only if there is an emergency. Understand?"

They understood. Once again they started for the strawberry patch. When they looked back to wave, Olmun was standing in the middle of the yard looking up at the mountains behind the house.

Olmun studied the mountainside from different angles. Then he went into the house, got his walking stick, and headed for the western slope.

Chapter 14

Now Olmun spent most of his time in the mountains on the west side of the valley. Whenever he left, he would remind them to ring the bell if there were an emergency.

Sometimes at meals he would ask, without seeming too curious, about the time they came into the valley. But they couldn't help Olmun. They remembered no more.

One day Olmun stopped going up the mountainside. He began telling and showing them more and more about the valley.

He showed them the account book. "Every day of every year since I came to the valley I have written in this book," he said as he turned the pages. "I kept track of the number of eggs gathered each day.

When crops were harvested I wrote the amount and where and how I stored them. Also the work done each day, like shearing sheep or repairing the pump."

Olmun handed the book to Talig. "I'd like you to take care of it. Do you think you can?"

Talig nodded. "I think so," he answered.

"Good," Olmun replied. "It should be done every day. You can start today, right after our middle-of-the-day meal. And something else. The calendar. Every day, at accounting time, tear off one sheet."

Olmun had them hitch the horses by themselves, and they rode to the fields in the wagon. There they practiced cutting the weeds at the edge of the field. He taught them how to sharpen the sickles and scythes on the grinding wheel.

He pointed out the different crops and talked about winnowing and storing the grain crops.

"For hay," he said. "We'll cut this field of grass." And he explained how to dry and bundle the hay. Later he showed them how to raise the bundles of hay into the loft of the barn with rope and pulley.

"If a rope wears thin or breaks, it can be spliced," Olmun said and demonstrated how to unwind each strand and then rewind the strands of the two pieces together.

"You can even make rope from linen fibers, if it comes to that. See how each strand is made of many fine fibers twisted together in the same direction?

Then those strands are twisted together in the opposite direction."

Rydeck and Talig practiced splicing rope.

Olmun took everyone to the orchard and pointed out the various fruit trees. "The apricots will be ripe first," he told them. He showed them the drying racks and explained how to prepare the apricots for drying and how to store them after they were dried.

He showed them how to extract the honeycombs from the beehives that stood square and wooden at the edge of a field of clover. To Shabin he gave that job.

In the garden, Olmun coached them until they knew the names of the vegetables. "Don't forget to let some of each vegetable go to seed," he said, "and don't eat green potatoes."

He showed them the wild raspberry bushes at the edge of the woods. "But," he warned, "don't eat anything that grows wild—berries or roots or leaves—without finding out first if it is safe.

"I can look it up in my book," Alew said.

They liked going around the valley with Olmun and learning about everything. Even Rydeck and Alew were willing to leave their weaving and pottery to go with Olmun.

At mealtimes Olmun asked questions about what they had learned, and they would shout and wave their hands until one was chosen to answer.

Talig wrote all these things in the account book.

Sometimes Olmun asked Talig to write only the names of the books in the study where they could find the information they needed. Always, though, there was something for Talig to write in the account book.

One day Talig said, "We don't have much paper left."

"I know," Olmun nodded. "There is more paper for the notebook in the middle desk drawer. When that is gone—." He paused. "As for making paper—wood pulp—but also chemicals. Flax, if we could spare enough. We'll experiment. But it takes time. We haven't finished our soapmaking experiment yet. And there will be other things that need replacing."

One day Olmun made an announcement. "I have found the place where you came into the valley." They made no comment, and Olmun continued, "Taking care of the valley requires a lot of hard work. In the early spring the garden and fields need plowing and planting and the weeds need to be kept down. In late summer, harvesting, storing, and preserving keeps everyone busy. But between early spring and late summer there is a bit of a lull."

Olmun looked at each of them. They did not seem to understand the meaning of what he said.

"I thought this would be a good time," he went on. "Before the apricots are ripe. Before the beginning of the busiest time. A good time for me to take a trip out of the valley."

Now they asked questions.

"Can we go too?" Meeja asked.

"Not now," Olmun told her. "I'll come back for you if it's safe. In the meantime you'll be safe here in the valley."

"How long will you be gone?" Talig asked.

"Not long. Two weeks." Olmun spoke directly to Talig. "Keep the calendar up to date. When two weeks are up—," his voice trailed off. "I have a plan. We'll talk about it later."

"When are you going?" Alew's voice quavered.

"I thought I would go when everyone knew everything about taking care of the valley. But there is always more to learn. I don't think I should wait. I think I should go tomorrow."

They all stared at Olmun. Rydeck said, "Tomorrow is too soon."

"But later will be too late," Olmun explained. "I want to get supplies and be back in time to start harvesting. And I want to find my children and grandchildren, if I can." He explained how his children and grandchildren were to have come to the valley, but the landslide closed the pass and he could not find another entrance.

"But now," he said, "I have found the way you came into the valley, and I think I should go."

Olmun looked at their worried faces. He tried to

sound cheerful. "Let's visit the valley this afternoon. We'll start with the sheep and Howler in the south and finish at the mill and the pond. How's that?"

But they weren't ready to go anywhere.

"Have you told us enough?" Alew asked.

Olmun thought awhile before answering. "Probably not. There's always more to learn. But there are books. And there are your own brains to think with." He smiled at them. "You will do very well. You each have special skills, and, what's most important, you work well together on big jobs. You help one another." He smiled at Pummy, "And Pummy helps everyone. Don't you, Pummy?"

She squirmed with pleasure. "Yes," she said, "and I can do everything."

Olmun rose from his place at the table. "Come. Let's tour the valley."

That evening, as they sat on the porch step watching the valley grow dusky, Talig asked, "Do we need some rules? I can write them down."

"Rules?" Olmun said. "Yes, I've thought of rules. I've thought of many, but I've decided there is only one that I want to tell you. That rule is: *no fighting.*"

"We won't fight," Shabin said. He sounded shocked. "We don't want to fight. Not anybody. Ever." The others nodded at Shabin's words.

"Someday you may," Olmun said. "That's why I'm telling you this rule: *no fighting.* I mean, no hurting one another."

They looked bewildered, and Olmun seemed sorry that he had said anything. Even so, he repeated, "Remember. It's important. No fighting."

Then he asked, "You'll go up the mountainside to the entrance with me tomorrow morning, won't you?" They said they would. "I have something to show you up there, something important."

They sat in silence and listened to the evening sounds. The chickens clucked softly while settling to roost. The leaves of the trees ceased rustling as the breeze died down. The valley became as still and silent as they. A planet shone near the faint crescent of the new moon visible in the western sky.

"Could we—," Shabin hesitated, then went on "could we sleep under the stars tonight?"

They gathered their blankets and brought them to the yard. They stretched out on the ground and looked up. Gradually the sky darkened and the stars appeared. They talked quietly, pointing out different constellations.

Before they grew too drowsy, Olmun told them, "I remember when I was searching and searching for this valley those many years. I thought I would never find it. But now I know I can always find my way back because I know exactly where it is."

As though to himself, he continued, "Once a person has lost something precious and then found it, he takes special care never to lose it again."

Chapter 15

With the first brightening of the sky, Olmun rose and began final preparations for his trip into the outside world.

One by one the others drifted into the house. They stared at his strange suit and the gas mask hanging around his neck. By the time he strapped on his knapsack they were all there.

"Are you ready to go up the mountainside with me?" he asked the silent children. "You can do your morning chores and eat breakfast later."

Olmun picked up his heavy walking stick and started toward the door. When they stepped onto the porch they heard howls coming from the meadow.

Olmun listened and then whistled loudly. Soon

Howler joined them. He sniffed at Olmun and whined and wiggled. Olmun patted him and said, "Come on, you can come with us to the entrance."

Before they left he said, "You can see the entrance from the yard. That is, you can see where it is, but you wouldn't be able to tell it is an entrance unless you already knew."

Olmun walked across the yard, almost as far as the barn, looked up at the mountainside, walked toward the house a few steps, and then moved slightly to his right. "This is the place," he said and made a deep grooved X in the hard-packed dirt with his walking stick.

They all took turns standing in that spot while Olmun told them where to look. "See the chimney? Now, look straight up from there. See that deeper colored part just over the treetops? I put a flag there. It's just a red dot from here. That's it."

After each one had seen the flag that marked the entrance, they started on their way. Though they had seen where they were going to go, once they left the spot Olmun had marked, they could no longer see the entrance.

"Pay attention to the way we go so you'll have no trouble on the way back," Olmun said as he led them toward the entrance. They climbed upward across streams, through stands of trees, and around boulders.

At last they stood on the ledge in front of the

entrance. They looked down at the valley below, and some them remembered the time they had seen it before.

Olmun talked about the strangeness of the entrance, that it had not been there before that he knew. It must have been made by a cracking and shifting of the mountain.

Finally he said, "Now I'm going to tell you something important." He moved some rocks at the back of the ledge and showed them a plastic-wrapped cord that he called a fuse. Out of a crevice above the fuse he took the waterproof container of matches that had been in Alew's satchel. Then his instructions began.

"If I do not return in two weeks, one of you should come up to the entrance, uncover the fuse, take the matches from the crevice, and light the fuse. As soon as it is lighted, run, as fast as you can, down the mountainside. There will be enough time to reach the house."

To be sure they understood, Olmun repeated his directions. Although they understood what they should do, they did not understand what would happen once the fuse was lighted.

Olmun explained. "After the fuse is lighted, after the one who lighted the fuse has reached the house, there will be an explosion. The only way into the valley will be closed."

They accepted what Olmun said. They trusted

him. They had always followed his instructions. So now they made no objections.

Olmun covered the fuse with rocks and returned the waterproof container of matches to the crevice. "There are only six matches," he told them. "They are not to be used for any other purpose than to light the fuse."

He smiled at the children who stood in a semicircle before him, but they only half smiled back. He shook hands with each one in turn.

When he reached Pummy, Olmun stooped down in front of her. Tears streamed down her face. "There, there," he said. "I'll be back."

He shook Howler's paw last of all and told him to stay. He had to say "Stay!" a number of times and finally asked Meeja to hold Howler firmly.

It was time to leave. Olmun squared his shoulders in a final, determined way and took one last lingering look at the valley below. "Take care of the valley. Take care of one another. And, remember, no fighting," he told them. Then he turned and disappeared between the two steep sides of the entrance.

They waited and watched the empty space where they had last seen Olmun. They half expected him to appear again. But he did not. After a long time Shabin said, "He's gone."

They trudged down the mountainside into the valley.

They ate breakfast and went off to do their chores.

After their middle-of-the-day meal, they sat on the porch step. This was the time Olmun had taken them places, showed them how to do different things, and talked to them. Now they did not know what to do without him.

Shabin finally said he thought he'd chop some wood and went off to the woodshed. Rydeck decided it was a good time to do some more weaving. Meeja asked Pummy to go with her to visit Howler and the sheep in the meadow.

After a while Alew said, "I think I'll go and see about the clay."

Talig, sitting on the porch step alone, leaned back against a post and did nothing.

The loneliest time was going upstairs to bed. They didn't talk as they usually did, but when they reached the top of the stairs, Pummy said, "I miss Olmun." Meeja, who was nearest to Pummy, gave her a hug.

The days that followed were much like the first day, the day Olmun left. Each one did his morning chores carefully. They took care of the valley as Olmun told them to do. After the middle-of-the-day meal and accounting time, each went a separate way. While they were busy, they didn't think about Olmun's being away. Each could imagine he was still in the valley, only somewhere else, helping someone else.

The only time they were all together was during meals, when each one talked about what he or she was doing.

Talig would say, "I've been experimenting, making cheese. What you have to do is—"

Shabin would say, "Today I chopped more wood than I ever chopped before in one day."

Rydeck talked about his weaving, and Meeja told how she was carving designs on the sides of her wooden clogs. Alew described her newly made bowl.

But no one listened to anyone else.

When Alew was ready to fire her clay bowl, she wasn't sure she could do it alone. Twice she asked Talig to help, but he was either busy reading or pressing cheese or doing something else.

One day, while they were eating their middle-of-the-day meal, Alew asked, "Can't someone help me fire the kiln?"

Rydeck was saying, "Where was everybody when the chickens got out? I had to chase them all by myself."

And Talig said, "The raspberries are ripe. You're all going to pick them with me, aren't you? How about you, Shabin?"

But Shabin wasn't listening. Instead of answering, he said, "I was thinking while I was chopping. Why did Olmun say, 'No fighting'? We never fight. We never will fight."

"Well," Talig said, "if no one will help, I'll pick the raspberries myself."

"And I'll fire my bowl myself," Alew said.

The meal was over and everyone left, except Alew.

Chapter 16

Alew took some hot coals from the stove with a pair of tongs, put them in a tin bucket, and carried them to the kiln. Then, with the tongs, she placed the hot coals in the midst of the charcoal on the grate. She blew on the coals until they glowed and turned to ash. Soon Alew felt heat coming from the kiln. It grew hotter and hotter.

Carefully, she slid the bowl onto the rack and shut the door with a smile of satisfaction. She waited awhile even though she couldn't see what was going on behind the closed door of the kiln.

Finally, with a feeling of contentment, she started for the garden, ambling along, enjoying the day, until something drew her attention. It was chickens.

Chickens were all over the garden, pecking at the plants.

Alew clapped her hands and ran toward them, shouting. Shabin heard her and came running. He shouted more loudly than Alew. The chickens squawked and flapped and scattered in every direction. The noise brought Rydeck from the weaving house. He also shouted and ran at the chickens.

Feathers flew as the chickens tried to escape. Some rose a few frantic feet and landed among the plants. Some half ran and half flew. Some skulked between the rows. All of them made noise and looked angry and ruffled.

Alew, Shabin, and Rydeck were ruffled too. They chased this way and that, shouting at the chickens and to one another. "Over there!" "Get that one!" "Shoo! Shoo!"

At last the chickens were all driven back into their yard. Just as Shabin was fastening the wire door behind the last chicken, Meeja and Pummy appeared. They had been in the meadow, and they were happy and laughing; each wore a garland of clover.

"Meeja," Shabin called angrily. "You let the chickens out again."

"No, I didn't," Meeja defended herself.

"You left the door open," Shabin accused. "You always leave the door open."

"No, I don't." Meeja said as she came closer.

"You're too careless," Shabin continued.

"I am not." Now Meeja was standing in front of Shabin, staring angrily at him.

Shabin stared back. "You're always letting the chickens out."

Meeja waved her arms and shouted. "Well, how would you like to be always locked up?"

Shabin held his ground. "How would you like to have nothing to eat?"

Rydeck and Alew did nothing but watch. Pummy screamed, "You're fighting! You're fighting!" She rushed at Shabin and Meeja and pounded them with her fists. "Stop fighting. Stop fighting."

Meeja dodged Pummy's fists. Shabin put his hand on her head and stood back, away from her swinging arms. Even though Pummy swung her arms harder, she couldn't reach anything to hit. She howled with rage and frustration.

"Pummy, Pummy. We're not fighting," Shabin said several times. He took his hand away from Pummy's head and held her arms. "Pummy, you're the one who's fighting."

Pummy's legs went limp, and she collapsed sobbing at Shabin's feet. Meeja knelt and put her arm around Pummy. "There, there, Pummy."

Pummy gulped and sobbed and hiccupped. "Olmun said," she sobbed and hiccupped again, "'No fighting.'"

"We weren't fighting," Meeja said. "Were we, Shabin? We weren't fighting."

Shabin stooped down. "We weren't fighting. We were just arguing."

Pummy looked from Shabin to Meeja with tear-stained eyes. "Is arguing all right?" she asked.

"I think so," Shabin said. Pummy still looked worried.

"Yes," said Meeja firmly. "Arguing is all right."

Just then Talig came and asked, "What's happened?"

They explained that Pummy thought Meeja and Shabin were fighting, but they weren't. They were only arguing. They stood in uneasy silence until Talig said, "I came because my pail was full of raspberries."

"Raspberries," Rydeck shouted. "Let's have some. Right now."

Alew and Meeja ran to the springhouse for cream while the others went inside to set the table with bowls and spoons.

It wasn't until the last plump, sweet-tasting berry had been eaten that Talig noticed the stove. He jumped up, shouting, "The damper's open." He dashed to the stove, but before he reached for the damper he stopped. He felt the stove. "The fire's out," he said. He lifted the lid, shook the grate, and watched the ashes fall through. "Nothing. Not one hot coal."

He turned to the others who were watching from their places at the table. "Who did it? I didn't do it. I always bank the fire. Olmun said to. I never leave the damper and draft open and go away."

No one answered because Talig didn't give any of them time. "I'm the one who's supposed to take care of the fire. Nobody else. Somebody left the damper and draft open." He glared at them. "Now there's no fire. What are we going to do? There aren't any matches."

"Oh, Talig," Alew said, tears streaming down her face. "I did it. I'm sorry. I took some fire to the kiln. But I left a lot. I thought I left enough."

"You also left the damper—." Talig looked more closely at Alew's tearful face and ended saying, "Don't cry. We'll do something. We'll start the fire again. Maybe we can use one of the matches Olmun left at the entrance."

"We can't take matches from the entrance," Shabin said.

"Just one," Talig argued. "There'll still be five left."

"No," Shabin insisted. "If we take one now, then we'll take one some other time. Olmun said not to take any."

Pummy had moved closer to Meeja. Meeja put her arm around Pummy who watched the others as they talked. Pummy whispered, "Are they fighting?"

"No," Meeja said as she patted Pummy's shoulder, "not really fighting."

They all heard Meeja's words and stopped talking.

"Is there fire in the kiln?" Rydeck asked Alew.

She was slow to answer. "Yes, but please don't take it. If the door is opened, the bowl will crack."

"But we've got to," Talig blurted. "We've got to have fire and—"

"Yes," Rydeck joined in. "What's worse? A cracked bowl or no fire?"

"A cracked bowl," Alew quickly retorted.

"No, it's not," Shabin said, "and you know it."

Now Alew's tears started flowing again. "But I'll never make another bowl. Nobody wants to get clay with me. Nobody even wanted to help me with the kiln." Alew stopped crying and became angry. "If Talig had helped, the fire wouldn't be out."

"It wasn't my fault," Talig clenched his fists in anger. "It was *your* fault. You did it."

"I asked you twice to help and you wouldn't," Alew shouted.

"Stop!" Shabin shouted, louder than both of them.

Talig and Alew stopped shouting, but they were still angry.

Meeja said, "We've got to have fire." Her voice rose higher as she talked. "We've got to sterilize the milk pails and the pans. We've got to cook—."

She looked at Pummy and her voice trailed off.

There was silence until Rydeck said, "I don't understand why you don't want us to get the fire from the kiln. You can make another bowl. Maybe this one won't even crack."

Alew only looked stubborn.

"We can just go and take the fire, whether she wants us to or not," Talig announced.

Alew opened her mouth to retort, but Shabin spoke first. "No. We can't do that. That would really be fighting. Alew has to say we can."

Now the silence was worse than the arguing. Alew glared at everyone, except Shabin. He glared at everyone, including Alew.

Pummy sat small and withdrawn, her face twisted in a worried frown. Suddenly she spoke in a high, clear voice. "Do you know what we never do anymore? We never play games." Pummy said, again in a pleading voice, "Can't we play a game? Together?"

"Yes, Pummy," Alew said slowly. "We can play, after we get the fire from the kiln."

Chapter 17

They got the fire. After the stove was warm and glowing with draft and damper set, they went outside, taking the biggest ball with them.

They played throwing games, then keep-the-ball-in-the-circle, no hands allowed. They shouted and ran, jumped up and down. Becoming hot, they decided to go to the pool by the waterfall.

When they were tired of swimming, they gathered on the grassy bank above the edge of the pool and stretched out contentedly, lulled by the splashing, gurgling water and soothed by the wavering sunlight through the leaves.

Alew was the first to break their silence. "Nobody will ever go with me to get clay. I just know it."

"Yes, we will," Rydeck promised.

"No. It's too far. It takes too long," Alew said. "You don't want to leave your weaving."

"If we could only go across the lake, instead of around it," wished Talig, "in a boat."

"We could never build a boat," said Shabin.

"Maybe not," Talig agreed, "but we could build a raft."

"It would take too long," Alew said, "longer than walking around the lake."

"But then we'd have the raft, and any time you wanted more clay, you could just go across the lake in the raft and get some."

That sounded better to Alew. "All right," she said, "but who knows how to build a raft? And who will build it?"

"I know how," Talig replied. "I saw a picture in a book. It's just logs fastened together, tied with rope."

"I can make the rope," Rydeck offered.

"I'll saw the logs," said Shabin.

"I can bring the horses to haul the logs," volunteered Meeja.

"It won't take long," Talig said.

But it did take long. Day after day they worked. Talking, planning, and deciding took the most time. After they finally agreed upon the length for the raft, they took turns sawing the logs. Then the horses dragged log after log to the grassy shore behind the weaving house. Together they cracked the crusty stalks away from the linen fibers, and each did some of the twisting and twining until enough rope was made. At last they were ready to put the raft together.

They began notching the logs. When the first two were ready, they rolled them into the shallow water, and everyone helped tie them together with rope. Then they each had to test the two-log raft by lying on it and paddling around.

"It won't take much longer," Talig said. Alew smiled.

They could do no more that day because the sun had almost set and darkness would soon be there. They tied a rope from the logs to the willow tree that hung over the lake and went to the house.

The next day, as soon as their morning chores were done, they started notching logs. But they had hardly begun when Pummy said, "I'm hungry."

"We ate," Talig told her.

"But not cooked food. We never have cooked food anymore. We never have bread or anything."

Even though Talig had kept the fire going in the stove, not one of them had taken time to cook after they began working on the raft. Nor had they had regular middle-of-the-day meals. They gobbled raw vegetables, eggs which they mixed in their milk, and cheese. The last batch of bread had been eaten some time before.

"I'll make some bread," Talig offered. "Come on,

Pummy. You can help." He headed for the house with Pummy skipping by his side.

"And butter too?" she asked.

"Yes, butter too," Talig said.

Meeja and Shabin notched the next log while Rydeck and Alew went to the woodshed for a pole. The rest of the morning Alew stood on the two-log raft that was still tied to the tree and practiced poling it back and forth. When the third log was ready, she stopped long enough to help tie it onto the first two. Then she climbed back on and continued poling.

The fourth log had just been rolled into the water when Talig and Pummy came with fresh bread, butter, and a jar of honey. The sight and smell of the bread was wonderful.

Alew scrambled up the bank, leaned the pole against the tree, and ran to help Talig and Pummy. Shabin, Meeja, and Rydeck let the log splash into the water as they too hurried to help.

They ate slice after slice of the warm brown bread, butter, and sweet honey. Talig went to the house for another loaf and more butter before they had eaten their fill.

As the last bite of bread disappeared, Meeja said to Talig and Pummy, "Another log's been tied on."

"And another one is notched and ready," Rydeck said. "Come see."

But they could not find the fourth log.

"Where is it? Where did it go?" Meeja demanded. "We put it in the water just when you came," she told Talig.

"It must have drifted away," Shabin said.

They stood on the bank and looked through the leaves of the drooping willow branches, but they could see nothing on the lake that looked like a log.

"Maybe it's along the shore farther down," Rydeck said.

They followed the shore line, sometimes on the grass and sometimes in the water. They worked their way past the barn and through the field where the horses and cows grazed, but they didn't find the log.

"It couldn't have gone this far," Alew said. "The water's so calm."

"But there's a current. I felt it," Rydeck said.

Pointing, Meeja shouted, "There it is!" The log was far from shore and gliding slowly southward toward the cliff where the water flowed underneath.

"We can't get it," Shabin declared. "It's too dangerous."

They walked along the shore and climbed over the fence that separated the field from the meadow in order to watch the log more closely as it floated farther south. When Howler ran up to greet them, they returned the greeting, but their attention was on the log. As they followed along the stone fence that kept the sheep from the water, they saw the log gather speed and hurry toward the cliff. They all gasped and held their breath. It reached the falls, upended, and dove under the cliff. They let their breath out in one loud sigh.

No one spoke until Shabin said, "That's what could happen to us on the raft."

"But," Alew objected, "we would have a pole. We wouldn't come this far south."

"It would be all right," Talig argued. "We'd stay north."

"No. It's too dangerous." Shabin stood in front of the others, arms folded.

Rydeck said, "Olmun didn't have a raft or a boat."

"Maybe he didn't get around to it," Alew said. "Like weaving and pottery." At the mention of pottery she paused, and said, "If we never finish the raft, we'll never get any clay. I just know it."

"But, Alew," Meeja cried out, "we don't want to go under the cliff like that log. That would be awful."

"Yes," Alew had to admit. She looked away from the rushing water, toward the northern end of the lake where the water was smooth. "But couldn't we? If we stayed north?"

"I think it would work," Talig said. "But maybe we ought to wait till Olmun comes back."

"Yes," Rydeck said. "Let's wait till Olmun comes. He'll help us."

"When's Olmun coming?" Pummy asked.

They couldn't answer Pummy's question. They didn't know how long it had been since Olmun had left. There had been no accounting of days since they'd started making the raft. No one had thought about the calendar, not even Talig.

Chapter 18

They said good-bye to Howler; each one patted him and told him he was a good dog. He whined and circled from one to the other, following them through the meadow until they reached the gate. Then he went back to the sheep.

When they entered the house, Talig went immediately to the calendar. "I know I didn't take off a page today, so I'll take it off now."

"Or the day before," Rydeck said. Off went another page.

"How long did we work on the raft?" Talig asked.

They started counting on their fingers and asking one another questions. What about the first day, the day they got the idea? Some thought Talig had taken care of the calendar that day and some thought he had not. Well, Shabin knew that to get the logs cut and down to the lake it took two days. But had it? Didn't they do something else besides move logs that second day?

Pummy said nothing but looked with interest from one to the other. Then she asked, "Are we arguing?" Everyone heard her and stopped talking. "Are we arguing?" she asked again.

"Of course not," Talig told her.

"What are we doing?" she asked. "When you say, 'I think so,' 'I don't think so,' 'Yes, it is,' 'No, it isn't,' what's that?"

"It's just talking," Meeja explained. "Maybe more than talking, but it's not arguing."

"It's discussing," Alew said. "It's not arguing, and it's not just talking and telling things."

"Yes," Rydeck agreed. "That's what we're doing. We're discussing. That's more than talking, but not as much as arguing."

Talig added, "After arguing comes quarreling."

They all agreed. That was the way it was—talking, then discussing, then arguing, then quarreling, which still wasn't fighting.

"And we won't fight," Shabin told Pummy.

They did reach an agreement about the calendar. Olmun, they decided, was due back that very day or the next. Maybe as late as the day after that, but very soon.

"Now," Alew said as she looked at the dirty

bread pans and the flour spilled on the floor, "we have to clean things up."

"I was busy churning butter," Talig said to explain why he hadn't cleaned up after himself.

They got busy. Shabin, Rydeck, and Pummy helped Meeja with the barn and the chicken yard. Talig and Alew cleaned the kitchen and eventually the rest of the house. They remembered the honey jar and butter crock that had been left by the lake and went after them.

"I wish—," Alew began when she saw the unfinished raft.

"I still think we could go north and be safe," Talig said. "Maybe when Olmun comes."

Talig tied the rope of the three-log raft around the tree more securely so it wouldn't float away. Then they went back to the house.

That night they worked as late as they could and then started immediately the next morning. They shined and polished, swept and weeded and straightened. The more they did, the more they saw that needed doing. But how much brighter and nicer everything looked! "Won't Olmun be glad?" they kept telling one another.

That second day Shabin said that he thought the apricots were ripe. But the others said they weren't. They tasted a few and decided to wait a day or maybe two days.

"I don't like apricots," Pummy declared.

"You will when they're ripe," Meeja told her. "They're sweeter then. I remember."

"I don't remember apricots," Alew said, "but I remember other things."

All that day they worked, and the next, and the day after that, cleaning and fixing and straightening and waiting, waiting for the apricots to ripen and for Olmun to come.

Once they went up the mountainside to the entrance to wait for Olmun, hoping he would come while they were there. But they didn't stay because Pummy cried.

"Where's Olmun?" she kept asking. "You said Olmun was coming."

"We only said that we hoped he would come," Talig tried to explain. But Pummy still cried. No one could make her understand or stop crying. So they left.

To amuse Pummy on the way back, they played follow-the-leader. Taking turns as leader, they jumped and hopped, waved their arms and waggled their heads, crawled and walked backwards, made faces, and fell down. Pummy finally stopped crying. They ran the rest of the way down the mountain into the valley.

The apricots ripened, but Olmun had not returned.

Chapter 19

When the apricots were ready, Shabin and Rydeck took out the drying racks, and they all started preparing the apricots for drying. They cut them in two and arranged them in rows as Olmun had told them to.

"Olmun said he'd be home before they were ripe," Meeja said.

"It's been more than two weeks," Rydeck added.

Shabin had just come with another basket of apricots. He set them down and said, "Someone should go up to the entrance and light the fuse. Olmun said so."

No one said anything. They thought about the fuse, about blowing the entrance shut, about what it would mean. They thought of all the questions they hadn't thought of the day Olmun left.

Meeja grew quite excited. "But Olmun could never come back."

"He could," Rydeck said. "He'd find a way."

She interrupted, "But we could never get out—never."

"Maybe we could find a way," Talig said.

"No, we couldn't," Meeja screeched. "We never could. Olmun could never get in. We could never get out. Don't do it."

"But Olmun said to," Shabin insisted.

"I'm going." Meeja dropped the apricot she still held in her hand and ran. "I'm going to go."

They ran after her, shouting, "Wait, Meeja! Meeja, don't go!"

She was a swift runner, and they never would have caught her if she had not turned to shout at them, "I've got to go. Don't stop me."

"Wait," Shabin called again.

"I'll find Olmun," she said. "I'll find him, and we won't have to blow up the entrance." While she was saying that, Rydeck caught up with her. The others were close behind.

"You need your suit," Talig said.

"And food," Alew added.

"No," Meeja answered.

They pleaded with her to wait and asked her to come back. Then they noticed that Pummy wasn't with them. They all went back down the hill to look for Pummy. Meeja too.

They found Pummy at the house, sitting on the porch step, hugging her doll. Tears streamed down her face. She looked accusingly at Meeja. "You were fighting."

"No. No, I wasn't," Meeja said. But Pummy hid her face behind her doll and would not listen. Meeja turned to the others, "It's just that—it's just that—." She searched for words. Finally she blurted, "I could find Olmun. We have to find Olmun."

"He could still get back," Talig said, "even if the entrance were closed."

"But we can't get out." Meeja pounced on the real reason for her fright. "That's it, that's it, we could never get out again. I want to go. Doesn't anybody else?"

"I don't," Alew said. "I don't ever. I remember and—oh, I don't even want to remember." Alew sat down on the step beside Pummy and sobbed. Pummy peeked out from behind her doll, reached over, and patted Alew, saying, "There, there," as the others had done to her many times.

"Why do you want to go so much?" Rydeck questioned Meeja. "Don't you like it here? Don't you like us?"

Meeja was shocked by his words. "I love it. I love it," she repeated, "and all of you and everything, but I have to go. I have to go before I can never go again."

"Olmun said to close the entrance if he didn't come back in two weeks," Shabin reminded her. "It's been longer than that. We have to do it. We have to do what Olmun said."

Meeja faced the three boys who were standing in front of the step. "Olmun didn't say we had to stay in the valley." She glared at them. "And I'm going."

She tried to run past them, but Shabin stood in her way. "I'll go with you," he said.

"But you don't want to go."

"No, I don't want to go," Shabin said.

"Then why should you?" retorted Meeja. "I can go alone."

"No, you can't go alone." Shabin sounded stern and gruff.

Talig had spoken little, but now he said, "I think we could get out of the valley if we wanted to, even with the entrance closed. We could find a way. Build some steps or a ladder or something."

They began to look interested, except Meeja who frowned and said, "I want to go now."

"All right, Meeja," Shabin said. "We will go. But only for three days. After three days the others must light the fuse, even if we are not back."

"I don't like it," Alew roused out of her silence. "I don't like it."

"Don't worry, Alew," Shabin told her. "We'll be back." He looked so grim and determined that no one doubted him.

So it was settled. The argument was over. Plans were begun.

They went to the barn together, to the far corner where the implements and harnesses were kept. Shabin took the lid off the metal drum. He looked at one suit and then another until finally he said, "This is mine."

"How can you tell?" Meeja asked as she started looking for her suit.

"My name is in it."

"Your name, Shabin?"

"My other name."

Meeja stopped and stared at him. The others stared, too. "What is your name?"

"It is Shabin," he said. "Shabin is my name now."

Meeja searched through the suits quickly until she came to the one she was looking for. "Yes," she said. "This was my name. But I will be like Shabin and not say. I will be Meeja while I'm in the valley."

Talig and Rydeck crowded up to the drum and looked for their suits. Pummy didn't understand what was going on, and Alew hung back on purpose.

"Do you think Olmun knows our real names?" Rydeck asked.

"You mean our other names," Talig said. Then he added, "Yes, I think he must know. And maybe he is looking for—"

"Yes," Rydeck grew excited. "And that is why it is taking him so long."

Alew spoke. "He won't find anything for me. There is nothing."

Rydeck's excitement faded, and he quietly put his suit back into the metal drum. Talig returned his, and Shabin put the lid on the drum.

They left the barn, Shabin and Meeja carrying their suits and gas masks.

On the way to the house Rydeck said, "I know now how Meeja feels. Olmun wanted to know what was outside, too. Maybe I should go with Meeja."

"I will go," Shabin insisted.

"But you don't want to."

"That is why I must go. I will see that we get back. I will do everything to see that we get back." Shabin said no more. No one could argue with him. So it was settled once again and for the last time. Meeja and Shabin were to leave the valley early the next morning.

Chapter 20

"May we use your satchel?" Shabin asked Alew that evening as he and Meeja made final plans.

"Somebody told me," Alew began. "I was told to always keep it. That it was important to keep it."

"But you gave it to Olmun, didn't you?" Meeja asked.

"Yes, but he didn't take it away," Alew explained. "Not far away. It's still here in the house."

"We won't take it," Shabin assured her. "Maybe there's another knapsack like the one Olmun took."

In the closet under the stairs, they found three knapsacks hanging on a wooden peg, smaller than the one Olmun had used. Meeja and Shabin each took one. They packed them with food and a jar of water.

Now they were ready. They would put on their suits in the morning.

"Are we going to sleep outside?" Pummy asked.

"No," Shabin answered. "I want to sleep in my room."

"You can sleep with me," Alew told Pummy.

"But I want everybody." Pummy looked at Shabin. "All together," she said.

Shabin gave in. They brought their blankets and got themselves ready for sleep out in the open. But it wasn't like the other times.

"I wish you weren't—," Alew began.

"I know," Shabin spoke before she could say more. "But we are."

Talig reminded Shabin of the list of supplies that they needed most, and Shabin assured him that it was in the knapsack.

Rydeck sat up, "Shabin. Shabin. I was thinking. I could go with you."

It was Alew who answered. "No. We need you here in the valley." After a pause she added, "We need everybody."

"Yes, stay here," said Talig. "You don't really want to go, do you, Rydeck?"

"Couldn't we all go?" Meeja asked. "Just for a little while? We don't have to go far. We don't have to stay long. Not even three days. I just want to, I just have to."

"No!" Shabin was emphatic. Again, "No."

"Can't we sing a song?" Pummy asked. They were startled into silence. Everyone had thought Pummy was asleep.

Talig started to sing the song about the valley. But his voice was not true enough to carry the tune without the help of Shabin's strong voice, and Shabin wouldn't sing. Nor would the others.

Pummy snuggled against Alew and fell asleep without a song.

Shabin did not sleep at first. He lay stiff, staring at the sky overhead until, at last, his eyes closed.

Toward morning when only a sliver of moon in the eastern part of the sky cast its light upon the valley, Alew slipped out from under her blanket. She stood quietly for a while to make sure she had awakened no one, then she went away.

Later, when she returned and was carefully settling herself under her blanket, Pummy whimpered. "Shh," Alew whispered. The others stirred.

In moments a terrible, deafening boom shook the valley.

They all awoke immediately. Meeja and Talig jumped up, glanced wildly here and there and started to run, first one way, then another. Alew put her arm around Pummy and sat still. Shabin and Rydeck, after a startled second, jumped up. Shabin quickly went to the X that Olmun had marked. "It's the entrance," he called to the others.

They could not believe Shabin's words and went

to look for themselves. "How?" Talig asked. "Did Olmun come back? Did he do it?"

Rydeck, standing on the X, scanning the tumble of rocks, answered, "It couldn't have been Olmun. He'd be here by now, with us. He said there'd be time."

When Meeja looked up over the chimney and tree tops, she screamed. "It is! It is! It's closed! It's shut!" Her hands came up in fists. She waved her arms and stamped her feet, and she screamed again. "I knew it. I knew it! You didn't want me to go. None of you. You did it. You're mean." She ran to her blanket, looking as though she would fling herself upon it. But, instead, she grabbed it and ran toward the barn, sobbing, "I hate you. I hate you."

Talig and Rydeck followed her calling, "Come back." "We didn't." "Meeja, please." "Don't be so mad."

Meeja didn't answer. She ran, her body stiff with anger, her jaw shut tight. At the barn she kicked away the doorstops and struggled to push the big doors shut, first one and then the other. She looked up only long enough to say, "Get out of my way," to Talig and Rydeck who stood near, pleading with her.

"Let her go," Rydeck finally said to Talig. "She'll get over it."

Those words had more effect on Meeja than all their pleading. "I won't get over it," she shouted.

"I'll never get over it. You're mean. All of you. You don't care about me. About what I want. It's always get the eggs, milk the cow, feed the chickens, latch the chicken yard. You just care about you." She glared at Talig. "It doesn't matter to you, being all shut up in the valley. You like being shut up. You like being shut up so much that you stay in the house all the time—"

Talig said, "Meeja, I never said—"

But she didn't hear. On and on she went. "—with your books and dumb poems and—"

Rydeck moved close to Meeja and said loudly, "Meeja, don't say such things. You can't mean them."

But Meeja didn't stop. She glared at Rydeck and shouted back. "You!" She raised her fists. Rydeck stepped back. "You and your stupid weaving! That's all you care about."

Before they could catch their breath, Meeja ran to the chicken yard and, in one last angry act, unlatched the door. Then she was back, slamming shut the barn doors while she screamed at them. "Don't anybody come near me—ever." Meeja shot the bolt in place, shutting herself away from the others.

Rydeck and Talig stood stunned. Talig muttered, "Staying in the house. What's wrong with that? I thought she liked my poems. Maybe nobody likes my poems. Maybe nobody likes *me*."

Rydeck said, "It isn't only weaving I care about."

Talig's hurt feelings changed to anger, anger against everybody and everything. Rydeck was nearest. He was saying, "I care about other things."

"No, you don't," Talig accused. "You always weave. You only stop to eat. All the time just weave. Weaving's stupid."

"Stop it! Stop it," Shabin shouted as he came running. It had all happened so rapidly and was so surprising that Shabin only now moved into action. "Stop it. You're both stupid."

"That's what I thought you thought," Talig shouted back. "Now I know. Glad you said it. I'm stupid. Everybody thinks I'm stupid."

Now Shabin was upon them. "Fighting's what's stupid."

"Well, you don't have to look at stupid me anymore," Talig went on. "I'm going." He marched off, away from the barn, northward. He didn't look back.

Rydeck lashed out at Shabin. "See what you did? Calling us stupid. You always think you're right. You and your no fighting. You made Talig—"

"Aaagh," Shabin growled. "Why don't you go—go—go weave!"

Rydeck took a step backward, turned on his heel, and left. But he had not gone far before he turned around to shout, "You and your chopping. You should talk. At least I don't always brag about how

126

much I do. Always counting. You've got more wood than anybody needs." Rydeck ran the rest of the way to the weaving house.

Alew, who still sat with her arms around Pummy, had not said a word. Now she cried out, "It's ruined. Everything's ruined. Nobody cares about no fighting. They just want what they want. They're stupid."

Alew looked for support to Shabin, but Shabin just stared at her.

"They don't care about the valley," Alew went on. "They don't care about no fighting. They don't care about what Olmun told us. But I do."

Instead of agreeing with her, Shabin said, "You have what you want. But Meeja doesn't. Now we are all enemies."

"I didn't fight," Alew insisted. "I'm not an enemy."

"Yes, you are. You caused it all." Shabin turned his back on her and walked toward the woodshed.

Alew collapsed, cringing as though she had been struck. Then she began to sob great, shaking, breathtaking sobs.

Pummy had watched everything with round, startled eyes, clinging to Alew all the while. Until the last, Alew had silently patted and comforted her. Now Alew was in need of comforting, and Pummy patted Alew's shaking back.

"There, there," Pummy said, but Alew didn't

stop. "Alew. Alew," she said more loudly. "Alew. I'm not an enemy."

Alew stopped crying and looked up, but her eyes did not focus on Pummy. "You should be. It's my fault. I did it. I thought—but now I'm everybody's enemy." Alew began crying again. She covered her face with her hands.

"I'm not anybody's enemy," Pummy said.

Pummy waited quietly beside Alew, but Alew did not say anything. She didn't look up, and she didn't stop crying.

Finally Pummy went away. She went northward in search of Talig.

Chapter 21

When Talig left, he didn't know where he was going. He only wanted to get away from those people who thought he was stupid.

He walked with stiff, pounding steps that shook his body. His anger made his head pound in rhythm with his jarring steps and one repeated word: *stupid, stupid, stupid.*

Over the bridge and up the road to the mill Talig marched. There he opened the sluice gate for no reason, then flung himself on the floor of the mill, cradled his head in his arms, and wept. At last, completely exhausted, he slept.

When Talig woke to the rumbling of the waterwheel, he wasn't sure where he was. As he slowly raised his head, he saw Pummy sitting cross-legged next to him, watching him. "I looked and looked for you," she told Talig.

He said nothing but rolled over on his back and shut his eyes. He listened to the sounds of the wheel turning and the water splashing. Pummy waited.

"I'd better close the sluice gate," Talig said.

"I'm hungry," said Pummy.

Talig ground some corn into meal and then shut the sluice gate. They took cornmeal in a sack to the pond where they mixed a little water with the meal in their cupped hands. It was cold and gritty and hard to swallow, but it was food.

Talig began to think of cornmeal pancakes. He remembered something he had seen in one of Olmun's books.

"I think I know how to make a fire," he told Pummy.

Together they made a fireplace of stones and gathered dried grass, twigs, and dead wood. Pummy followed Talig around while he searched for a bent stick, a straight stick, two small slabs of wood, and a heavy string from a sack of grain. She watched as he assembled the pieces and then tried to make enough heat by friction to cause shreds of dry grass to catch fire. Pummy kept watching and Talig kept trying.

After a long time the wood looked scorched and smelled hot. There was a trickle of smoke, that was all. The tinder had barely burned before going out.

"I have to go now," Pummy said.

Talig hardly heard her. He was much too busy with his fire. Without saying more, Pummy left.

Much later, Talig started a fire. He had the right amount of dried grass at the right place at the right time and he managed to feed the small fire quickly enough so it did not go out, but not so quickly that it was smothered.

Not until the tiny flames had grown into a proper fire did Talig feel pleased. He sat back and wished Pummy were there to see it.

Maybe I'm not so stupid after all, he thought. Wait till they see. They'll say—

All at once Talig realized that they would not see his fire. They would never come. They would never know he wasn't stupid.

That's all right, he decided. I can get along. I have built a fire. Now I can make pancakes. And I can grind all the flour I want.

He remembered the almost-empty flour bin in the kitchen of the house in the valley. They'll need flour, he thought. When they come to get it, I'll say, "No flour. This is my place. Get out."

He liked that idea. But then he decided it would be better to say, "You can have flour, if you bring me milk and eggs."

He thought of Meeja locked away in the barn. Only she would have milk, and she had said she never wanted to see anybody again. Poor Meeja.

Maybe they'd just go and take the milk. Maybe they'd just come and take the flour. Maybe he'd better lock the mill and guard it.

Then Talig remembered a far-off time with many locks on doors and guards everywhere and no going anywhere without them. No. He wouldn't lock the door. Besides, there was no lock on the mill door.

He would just stay where he was, alone, until somebody came and apologized.

He sat beside his fire, keeping it alive, doing little else except gathering wood now and then.

He made up a poem:

> "Nobody comes, nobody cares,
> Nobody talks, nobody listens, no-
> body shares,
> The sun doesn't shine."

Talig looked around. The sun was shining. He changed the last line of his poem to:

> "The sun shines, but the valley is dark."

Chapter 22

Pummy left Talig in search of food and something more interesting to do than watch him with his sticks.

As she drew nearer the center of the valley, her steps slowed. Everything was quiet. She stopped on a rise overlooking the yard that separated the house and barn, but neither saw nor heard anyone. Slowly she walked on.

A flicker of brown in the garden caught her attention. It was a chicken. Now Pummy crept away from the garden toward the weaving house where the door stood open. At last she reached it and scurried inside, but the weaving house was empty.

She didn't want to go outside where the chickens lurked. She wished someone were there. She poked her head out the front door but saw no one. She

closed the door and sat on a bundle of wool in the corner.

Maybe everybody went away on the raft, Pummy thought. She went to the back window and looked out. There, at last, she saw someone. It was Rydeck.

Pummy opened the window and called, "What are you doing?"

"I'm making rope," Rydeck told her.

"I'm hungry."

"Go to the garden. That's what I do," Rydeck said.

"I can't. There're chickens."

"Oh, all right, but wait till I fix this." Rydeck wrapped some fibers around the end of the strand he was working on, went around the house, and opened the door for Pummy.

"You go," she said.

"No, come along, the chickens won't hurt you. They'll run away when you get near. You'll see."

They pulled up some carrots and picked some green beans. Staying close to Rydeck, Pummy carefully watched the chickens. They did go away whenever she came near. She grew braver. Once she walked right toward a chicken, and it scurried away. It wasn't as it had been in the chicken yard when they had come pecking and poking around expecting to be fed.

"You can wash these in the lake," Rydeck said as they left the garden. "And I'll show you my rope.

I'm starting the second strand. It's long, awfully long."

As soon as they were back, while Pummy was still washing her vegetables, Rydeck began twining rope. He fastened a bundle of fibers through the belt of his tunic, and began to walk backwards, adding fibers and twisting them together. When finished, the rope would stretch from the tree where the raft was tied to the edge of the weaving house.

Pummy munched a carrot as she watched. "Aren't you going to weave anymore?"

"No," said Rydeck. "It's stupid to weave all the time. But maybe rope-making isn't so stupid. Besides, it goes faster. Look how long it is. I did all that today and this much more."

Pummy sat with her feet in the water while Rydeck twisted more and more rope. When the afternoon shadows grew long, he asked Pummy where she was going to sleep. Pummy looked around at the growing darkness and said she thought she'd stay there.

Rydeck fixed a place for her on a soft mound of wool in a corner of the weaving house. He put a bundle of wool in front of the door for himself.

"Why are you sleeping there?" she wanted to know.

"Just because I feel like it, I guess."

"I looked at your weaving," Pummy said. "It's nice."

"Well, it's stupid. Go to sleep. Tomorrow I'm going to make more rope. Finish it, maybe."

Before falling asleep Rydeck said, "I'm glad you like my weaving."

The next morning he was busy with his rope before Pummy woke. When Pummy told him she was hungry, Rydeck asked her to wait until he had finished more of the strand he was making. "It takes three strands to make rope," he explained. "I want to make the longest rope in the valley. It'll be longer than any other rope."

Pummy waited, but it didn't seem as though Rydeck would ever stop and go with her to the garden.

Finally, she said, "I have to go now." She had heard the distant sound of ax against wood.

Rydeck heard it too. "Stupid chopping," he muttered.

Pummy left, and Rydeck continued his rope-making.

Chapter 23

Pummy went to the garden, keeping watch for chickens as she went. One and then another scurried away as she drew near. Pummy wasn't afraid of them anymore. She picked some vegetables and listened to the steady chopping sound that came from the woodshed.

The chopping ceased, and with her hands full of vegetables, Pummy headed for the woodshed, a chicken right behind her.

Pummy stopped and looked at the chicken. The chicken stopped, stood sideways, and looked at Pummy with its glassy, blinking eye. She walked backwards, watching it. The chicken didn't move, so Pummy turned around and walked toward the woodshed.

But now the chicken followed her. Pummy

stopped. The chicken stopped. Pummy started. The chicken started. Pummy ran, screaming, "Shabin! Shabin!"

Shabin came running. Pummy ran to him, wrapped her arms around his waist, and hid her face. "A chicken's chasing me," she sobbed.

Shabin patted her, saying, "There, there. Chickens don't chase people." He made her look. The chicken had stopped to peck at one of the green beans Pummy had dropped. "She thought you were going to feed her."

Shabin looked hungrily at the vegetables Pummy held. "You can wash them in the stream," he said.

They went past the woodshed to the stream on the far side. Pummy kicked off her clogs, waded into the water, and washed the carrots she carried. Shabin sat beside the stream and watched her.

"Do you want a carrot?" Pummy asked.

"Thank you," Shabin said as he accepted the carrot.

He ate his carrot slowly while Pummy munched carrot after carrot and green beans between times. "Don't you eat?" she asked.

"Just raspberries. That's all that's near."

"Have some more carrots," Pummy offered.

"No, they're yours," he said.

But Pummy had brought more than she needed and kept offering vegetables to Shabin. Finally, he accepted.

They sat side by side quietly eating. A faint trickling sound came from the stream.

"I heard you chopping a little bit but you stopped. Don't you chop anymore?"

"No," Sabin answered. "We have enough wood. Besides, the fire's gone out. There wasn't any smoke from the chimney yesterday or this morning."

"Talig's making a fire," Pummy said.

"Is he?" Shabin sounded interested. "Probably read about it in one of those books. He's smart."

"Talig says he's stupid."

Shabin stiffened. "Yes. Anybody who fights is stupid."

Pummy was startled by his gruff words. "I don't fight."

Shabin didn't pay any attention to her. "Now see how it is?" he continued. "It's worse than fighting. Everybody is everybody's enemy. Alew doesn't have any fire. I don't have any food except raspberries."

"You could go to the garden."

"No. Rydeck goes there. I don't want to see him. I don't want any more fighting." Pummy squirmed as Shabin continued. "How dare they fight? It's Olmun's valley. They ought to do what he says."

"I think I have to go now," Pummy said.

Shabin said nothing. He stared straight ahead, his jaw set, his back stiff, his eyes angry.

Pummy left. To avoid the garden and the

chickens, she walked behind the woodshed, along a path on the hillside above the orchard. The sound of strong, steady chopping from the woodshed started. But before long it stopped and the valley was quiet once again.

Pummy walked slowly and stopped often. She picked raspberries, waded in a stream, wandered through the orchard where she ate some apricots, and climbed a low-branched tree.

It was late afternoon before she neared the house.

When Pummy reached the corner of the house, she saw five mounds scattered about the yard. She waited. They didn't move, so they weren't chickens. Then she knew what they were—blankets, five blankets that nobody had picked up.

Pummy gathered a blanket in her arms and headed for the house. The front door, which usually stood open, was closed and Pummy had never opened it. She knocked, but no one came. When she tried the handle with both hands, the door unlatched and swung open.

There seemed to be no one in the house. Then she saw Alew sitting on a bench with her head on the trestle table, asleep.

Alew awoke, looked at Pummy through puffy eyes, then buried her head in her hands and cried.

"Here's your blanket," Pummy told her. Alew didn't even look up.

Pummy wandered around, felt the cold stove,

and peered into the cupboard. She found part of a loaf of bread and a hunk of cheese, took them to the table and offered them to Alew. Still Alew did not look up. Pummy ate bread and cheese in silence.

Finally Pummy asked, "Do you cry all the time?"

Alew took her hands away from her face. "Yes."

"Why?" Pummy asked.

"I'm everybody's enemy. Nobody likes me. Everybody hates me."

"Not me." said Pummy.

Alew went on talking as though Pummy had said nothing. "All I wanted was for us to be together. To not have anything bad happen. To not have anybody go away and not come back. But now it's awful. It's terrible. If only Meeja hadn't wanted to go."

Alew sniffed and wiped her eyes. "Now I feel like Meeja. I want to go. I hate it. Everybody hates me. I didn't mean it to be like this."

Pummy listened while the words poured forth. Alew talked about her clay and Rydeck's weaving and why people shouldn't do what they liked. People had to do things together too. But what if somebody wanted to do something that spoiled everything, like Meeja did?

Alew ended up saying, "But it wasn't Meeja who spoiled everything. It was me." She stopped talking and stared gloomily ahead.

Pummy looked around, saw the open door and

the yard beyond. She went outside, saw the rest of the blankets, and started bringing them into the house. Each time she came in, she said, "Here's a blanket." But Alew said nothing.

Finally, Pummy didn't return to the house. She took the last blanket and went away, leaving Alew silent and staring.

But Alew was not just staring, she was thinking. Her mind had been wrapped up tightly in sorrow. Now it began to move, stretch, and think. She thought about the day they had walked around the lake together. She remembered the little sand beach. She remembered the clay. She remembered Olmun asking if anyone recalled coming into the valley on that side of the lake.

Olmun had said that he'd looked for a way out of the valley, but maybe he hadn't looked in the right place. Maybe, with his sore foot, he couldn't climb around as well as she could. Maybe she should go and look.

Alew thought about walking past the weaving house, past the garden, and over the bridge to the other side of the lake. She decided she could not do that. Somebody might see her.

Then she remembered the raft. She could go very early in the morning past the north end of the barn to the tree where the raft was tied. That was the way, she decided. Rydeck wouldn't see her if she were very quiet and went very early in the morning.

Alew reached across the table for what was left of the bread and cheese. She thought about her plan as she ate.

Yes, she said to herself, that's what I'll do. Talig said that going north and staying near the shore would be safe. I'll land the raft on the little sand beach. Then I'll start searching. I'll stay there until I find a way out of the valley.

Alew was so pleased with her plan that she could no longer sit still. Her thoughts raced on. When I find a way out, I'll come back and tell everyone. Meeja can go then if she wants. Nobody will be mad anymore. They'll say, "Good for you, Alew. You're our friend."

Alew looked around for Pummy. She wanted to share her wonderful plan. But Pummy was gone.

Chapter 25

After Pummy picked up the last blanket, she stood and looked around awhile. She looked at the barn with its great doors shut tight. She started northward, but soon turned around and headed south instead.

When she reached the rail fence that enclosed the sheep's meadow, she stopped. She had never opened the gate by herself. With the bulky blanket she couldn't climb over because she had to hold it in both arms.

While she was standing, thinking about what to do, someone said, "Pummy, what are you doing here?"

Pummy was startled and turned around. It was Meeja who had come up so silently behind Pummy that she had not heard a sound.

"I'm looking for some place to be," Pummy said.

"Don't you have a place to go?" Meeja asked.

Pummy shook her head.

"It's getting late," Meeja said. "I'll show you a place to sleep."

Pummy followed Meeja away from the meadow and back toward the barn. They went behind the barn and through a small door. Not much light could get inside with the big doors closed, and it was dark.

Meeja led Pummy to the ladder. "I fixed a place in the loft," Meeja explained. "I'll carry your blanket."

In the loft, hay had been moved about to form a small roomlike place. In one corner of this space a small mound of hay was shaped like a bed.

"This will be a good place for you," Meeja said.

"Aren't you going to sleep here too?" Pummy asked.

"No," Meeja told her. "It's too small. It's too closed in. I made it but I—"

"Where do you sleep?"

"I—well, I just go out in the field, with the horses. They don't sleep much. They walk around and graze. Once in a while they stand still. I just stay on their backs. Do you want to do that?"

"No, they're too high. Can't we sleep with the sheep? They're not so high."

"Don't you want to stay here? It's a nice bed."

"I want to be with you," Pummy said.

"Well, come along. I have to find my blanket first. I think I left it here." Meeja found her blanket rolled up beneath the hay.

By the time they were out of the barn again the day's light had begun to fade.

Meeja walked slowly. Pummy sometimes went ahead of her, but not too far. They reached the meadow, and Meeja found a boulder that was warm from the sun. They stopped there. Howler came to see them and stayed for a while.

Meeja looked at the soft grass. "This will be better than a horse's back," she decided. "Wrap up well, Pummy." Then Meeja wrapped herself in her blanket.

The valley was quiet. "I never hear anything anymore," Pummy said. "Not the cows, not Howler, not the horses. Only Shabin chopping a little bit—twice."

"I take care of the animals so they don't have to call to be taken care of," Meeja explained. "I don't hear anything either. Just chopping, twice. Not even the chickens."

They listened to the quiet and soon fell asleep.

Just as the sky was beginning to lighten, Pummy woke because she heard a noise, a groan. Then more low, steady, anguished groans.

Meeja, wrapped tightly in her blanket, stiff and unmoving, groaned and gasped again and again.

Now there were muffled cries. "Help! Help! I can't move. I can't move."

Meeja's blanket was twisted about her body, and her head was covered. "I can't move," she cried out once more. But she didn't try.

Pummy, not fully awake, stood up. She took a step toward Meeja, tripped on her blanket, and landed on top of her.

Meeja moaned, "I'm being crushed. I'm being crushed. I can't move." Then she screamed, "Let me out! Let me out! Help me! Help me!"

Pummy grabbed at Meeja's blanket, but Meeja had started to move. She wiggled and squirmed and rolled over and thrashed about. Pummy scrambled away, clear of the violent motions. Meeja fought with the blanket, screaming, "Let me out!"

At last she was free. "Oh," she groaned as she looked into Pummy's frightened face. "Oh, oh. I thought—I dreamed—it was awful. It was just like before. Now I remember how it was."

Meeja closed her eyes and sat shaking. After a while she opened them, breathing deeply. "But it isn't the same." she said. "It's all right." She stood up and looked around the meadow, then back at Pummy.

"There's lots of room in the valley, isn't there?" Meeja asked.

Pummy nodded.

"There's lots of room," Meeja continued. "It's

not like—. No, it's not. I can move. I can run. Oh, I can run. Come on, Pummy, let's run."

So they ran, down the slope, across the grassy field, up and down the gentle dips, around the grazing sheep, and back up the slope. There they collapsed, laughing and panting.

Chapter 26

About the time Meeja and Pummy were running in the meadow, Alew woke in her bedroom.

After Alew had made her decision the day before, she began to prepare for the coming day. She straightened and cleaned the house, put the blankets back on the beds where they belonged, and then went to sleep in her own room.

The first brightening of the sky awakened her. Without hesitation she slipped out of the house, skirted the barn, and quietly made her way to the shore of the lake. Carefully she stayed behind the tree that stood between the shore and the weaving house. She found the pole still leaning against the tree, untied the rope, and pulled the raft through the water until it reached the shore.

Standing on the raft, she put one end of the pole

into the shallow water and pushed. The first push sent the raft gliding away from the shore. The second made it twist off course. Alew pushed again from another place.

"Alew," Rydeck shouted from a window of the weaving house.

Alew sat down so she would not fall.

Rydeck called again, "Alew. What are you doing?"

Alew stood up again and concentrated on making the raft go in the direction she wanted. She had to hurry. She didn't want Rydeck to stop her.

He was now calling from the shore. "You can't go. It's too dangerous."

Alew took time to say, "Talig said this way would be all right."

"Talig doesn't know. Come back."

But Alew was not going back. She poled the raft as quickly as she could, balancing carefully as she stepped from side to side. She had found a rhythm and was doing well. But she could do nothing else. She couldn't answer Rydeck. She had to pay attention to the raft only.

He stood on the shore watching her move farther away. "Alew, please. Before it's too late. Come back. Come back."

Alew paid no attention to Rydeck. She would go to the other side of the lake. She would find a way out of the valley.

Alew heard no more from Rydeck on the shore because he was no longer there. Rydeck was running to the house. There, he found no one. Where was Shabin? Where was Pummy?

Rydeck ran to the barn and hesitated a moment at the latched doors. Then he pounded on them. No one came. He turned to run. Where was everyone? at the woodshed? Then he remembered the bell.

Quickly he unfastened the rope and let it up—clang—and pulled it down—clang. The sound rang out across the valley. Again and again Rydeck pulled the rope.

Meeja and Pummy heard the bell and came running from the meadow. Shabin, who was still asleep in the small dark room at the end of the woodshed, woke, jumped up, and hurried toward the house. Talig heard the bell at the north end of the valley but had a much longer way to run. Before he reached the house, he saw the others running toward him.

"It's Alew," Rydeck shouted. "She's taken the raft."

"The current," Meeja gasped.

"Rydeck's got a rope," Shabin put in.

Talig joined them and they all ran together. At the bridge they paused to look for the raft and Alew, but the lake was too far and the trees too dense.

On they ran, up the path. Now they were single file, Meeja leading the way.

When they reached the part that skirted the steep cliff, they slowed a little and Meeja stopped to peer over the edge. She saw the raft directly below them. Alew was clinging to the side of the cliff with both hands, the raft bumping against the side of the cliff.

Meeja dropped to her knees and cautiously leaned out over the cliff. "Are you all right?"

"No," Alew's voice quavered. "I lost the pole. I can't hang on."

Now they were all on their hands and knees looking down at Alew. But she no longer looked up. Her hands grasped the side of the cliff, her feet braced to hold the raft from drifting away.

"Move along," Talig told her, "with your hands. There's a place to grab." Alew couldn't seem to move. "Go ahead," he urged.

Alew moved her right hand along the cliff wall and grasped a ridged place. Next she moved her left hand, then her right. Slowly she and the raft inched along.

"We can't throw the rope to her here," Rydeck said.

"No," Shabin agreed. "She couldn't catch it."

Rydeck stood up and hooked the coil of rope over his shoulder. "Down at the little sand beach—"

Shabin knew what Rydeck meant. "Tie it to the pine tree."

"And tie the other end to me," Rydeck said, "and I'll swim out—"

"And I'll haul you both in," Shabin finished.

Even as they spoke, Shabin and Rydeck were stepping over the kneeling bodies and running toward the little sand beach.

Meeja was saying, "Just a little way, Alew. There's another place. There. That's it."

"Be careful," Talig warned. "Don't let the raft drift out."

Alew's wavering voice floated up to them. "I can't. I can't." But she did. Slowly, while Meeja and Talig guided her, Alew and the raft inched along the cliff wall.

Pummy watched and listened. She gasped and sighed and held her breath when the others did, but said nothing.

They continued to inch along, Alew on the raft, Meeja, Talig, and Pummy on the path above. Then they reached the place where the path climbed upward, away from the edge of the cliff. They craned their necks, leaned out as far as they dared, and helped Alew as long as they could. She looked back at them in desperation; they stared down at her helplessly.

"Don't let go," Meeja pleaded.

"Hang on," Talig urged. "Shabin and Rydeck are coming."

Then, just for an instant, Alew loosened her grasp, and the raft slid away. She clawed at the cliff, lost her balance, and fell into the water.

The raft floated away, toward the south, toward the dangerous place where the water disappeared underground.

Alew surfaced near the cliff wall. She reached toward it but the current carried her away. She stroked and stroked, but the distance between her and the safety of the cliff widened. Alew gradually slipped southward behind the raft.

Alew fought against the current with fast, desperate, churning strokes. She spluttered, gasped, and sank below the surface. She rose again, still thrashing, still trying, still being carried southward.

Now another head bobbed beside Alew's and another pair of arms thrashed in the water.

"I've got you," Rydeck shouted as he wrapped his arms around Alew's body. Both Alew and Rydeck drifted toward where the water rushed under the cliff.

Shabin stood in the water near the sand beach grasping the rope. "Help me," he called, as Meeja and Talig came running up with Pummy right behind them. "Hitch up the slack to the tree. Now pull." They pulled and pulled, all of them.

Slowly Alew and Rydeck were drawn out of the mainstream toward the weaker, eddying currents.

At last they were safe. They crawled onto the sand and lay exhausted. Shabin untied the rope from around Rydeck's heaving chest and rubbed his cramped arms.

Alew choked and coughed and sobbed. Meeja helped Alew by pounding her back.

As soon as Alew could talk, she blurted, "I'm sorry. I'm sorry." Then, between sobs, she said, "I'm so awful. I make so much trouble."

"Alew," Meeja scolded, "don't say such things."

Alew frowned at her. "It's all my fault. I did it. I blew up the entrance, and you wanted to go so badly and I—" Alew's body shook with a sob.

Meeja threw her arm around Alew's shaking shoulders. "That's all right. I don't need to go. I'm not afraid of being closed up in the valley anymore. You just did what Olmun said. It's all right. Don't cry."

Pummy began to cry.

"Why are you crying?" Talig asked.

"Because. Because I didn't cry before."

Meeja started to cry too. "Oh," she wailed. "It was awful. I hate hating."

"Don't everybody cry," Talig pleaded.

Paying no attention to the crying, Rydeck said, "I'm glad I made that rope. I thought maybe it was stupid to make such a long one. But I guess it wasn't."

"You're not stupid." Shabin's voice was husky. "Nobody's really stupid. Only when they fight. I was stupid. I said—"

"Let's never fight again," Meeja interrupted. "Let's forget all about it. We can be the way we

157

were. And let's pretend that it never happened."

"No," Alew was emphatic. "No. We've got to remember. We can't forget how awful. How terrible. If we remember, we won't ever fight again."

They silently thought about her words.

"Do you know what I'm going to do?" Meeja asked. "I'm going to carve, all over everything—the porch, the posts, the barn. I'm going to carve: No Fighting. So we'll never forget."

"Yes," Shabin said. "We have to remember."

They rested on the beach in the quiet cove, happy that they were all together again. One of them sighed, then another. They were still, as still as the quiet water and the silent sun shining upon them.

Pummy was the first to stir. "Now what'll we do?" she asked.

"Go back," Meeja told her.

They started on their journey home. On the way they stopped at the pond.

"Shall we get some clay for you, Alew?" Rydeck asked.

Alew looked pleased, but she said, "Not now. Someday. When the harvest is over."

"But you like to work with clay so very much," Meeja objected. "I'll carry some for you."

They all scooped up some clay to carry to the valley for Alew while she carried the rope.

When they reached the path overlooking the

lake, they stopped again. Below them lay the valley, beautiful and inviting. They could see the house, the barn, the garden, the many sparkling streams, the fields, the horses, the meadow where Howler tended the sheep—everything.

Talig recited his poem:

> "There is a valley
> Where many streams flow
> And many things grow
> And people are friends."

Then he added another line:

> "No one knows where."

Alew said, "But Olmun knows where."

"Yes," they all agreed. "Olmun knows where."

lake, they stopped again. Below them lay the valley, beautiful and inviting. They could see the house, the barn, the garden, the many sparkling streams, the fields, the horses, the meadow where Howler tended the sheep—everything.

Talig recited his poem:

> "There is a valley
> Where many streams flow
> And many things grow
> And people are friends."

Then he added another line:

> "No one knows where."

Alew said, "But Olmun knows where."
"Yes," they all agreed. "Olmun knows where."